L-181

Erin Collins's Surefire Plan To Get Her Man To Remember Her:

♥ Whip out the old albums. He can't dispute photographic evidence.

♥ Ask him to move in...again. Maybe familiar surroundings will help jog his memory.

♥ On Valentine's Day, deliver him a 7 lb., 2 oz. beautiful baby girl.

WARNING: Amnesiac dads-to-be are especially hard to convince. Proceed with caution—and lots of love.

Dear Reader,

"What should I give my sweetheart for Valentine's Day?" women ask as February 14 draws near. Bestselling author Marie Ferrarella offers a one-of-a-kind gift idea: *The 7 lb., 2 oz. Valentine*—which is also book three of her wonderful cross-line series, THE BABY OF THE MONTH CLUB.

In *The 7 lb., 2 oz. Valentine*, Erin Collins is a mom-to-be, but the unknowing dad-to-be hasn't been seen in months. And when he does turn up, he doesn't remember *anything*—let alone her! Next month, look for book four of THE BABY OF THE MONTH CLUB series in Silhouette Desire.

Lori Herter, one of *Yours Truly*'s launch authors, presents her own valentine to you—*How Much Is that Couple in the Window?*—book one of her irresistible new miniseries, MILLION-DOLLAR MARRIAGES. Jennifer Westgate has to live in a department store's display window with a make-believe husband—for an entire week of newly wedded bliss! Look for book two of this fun series in August.

Next month, you'll find two *Yours Truly* titles by JoAnn Ross and Martha Schroeder—two new novels about unexpectedly meeting, dating...and marrying Mr. Right!

Happy Valentine's Day!

Melissa Senate
Editor

Please address questions and book requests to:
Silhouette Reader Service
U.S.: 3010 Walden Ave., P.O. Box 1325, Buffalo, NY 14269
Canadian: P.O. Box 609, Fort Erie, Ont. L2A 5X3

MARIE FERRARELLA

The 7lb., 2oz. Valentine

SILHOUETTE YOURS TRULY™

Published by Silhouette Books
America's Publisher of Contemporary Romance

To
Jeannette Stacey,
who was a
7 lb., 2 oz. almost Valentine herself.
Welcome to the world, Jeannette.

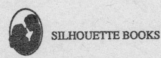 SILHOUETTE BOOKS

ISBN 0-373-52013-1

THE 7 LB., 2 OZ. VALENTINE

Copyright © 1996 by Marie Rydzynski-Ferrarella

This edition published by arrangement with Harlequin Books S.A.

Printed in U.S.A.

About the author

Hi!

I'd say that we have to stop meeting like this, except that I *love* meeting like this. It means you've picked up another one of my books to read. This one comes in the middle of THE BABY OF THE MONTH CLUB series and centers around a simply worded personal ad: "Brady, come home. Love, Erin." Simply worded things are usually the best. They go straight to the heart of a matter, and this did for me, when I thought of it.

I've been writing (simply and otherwise), since I was eleven. But mentally, I've been spinning stories since I was old enough to string two sentences together. Television was a huge influence. For instance, did you know that the Cartwright boys of "Bonanza" had a sister? (That's okay, they didn't know it, either.) Her name was Kit. Marty of "Spin and Marty" had a sister (I can't remember her name, so I guess she wasn't very impressive.) Zorro had one, too, (Zora— I was very young at the time and not overly creative.) In each case, the heroine was feisty, brave and wonderful, and yes, she was me. Writing myself into the stories always made them that much more exciting for me.

I never lost that time-worn tradition. A piece of me, of my heart, is in each heroine, each story, I write. That's why they're always so special to me. So here I go again, offering you my heart wrapped up in a story of love lost and then found. I hope it succeeds in giving you a little pleasure.

Love,

Marie

BRADY AND ERIN LOCKWOOD

ARE

PROUD TO

ANNOUNCE THE

BIRTH OF THEIR

PERPETUAL

VALENTINE,

JAMIE

1

Brady, come home. I love you, Erin.

Nerves that would have put a well-rehearsed chorus line to shame danced all through her, doing triple time. Erin fingered the ad she had placed in the personals column of the *Times*.

Maybe touching it would bring her luck.

The scrap of newspaper lay deep within her purse. It was the first of a series that had appeared faithfully in the newspaper four Fridays in succession. When she'd phoned the ad in, Erin had known that the odds against Brady's even seeing it were incredibly small. The Brady Lockwood she knew never looked at such things.

But desperation drives you down unorthodox avenues, and Erin Collins had been desperate. Desperate to find Brady, to see him just one more time. Not because he was the father of her unborn child, but because he was Brady and she loved him.

She had to know that he was all right before she could go on with the rest of her life.

So when the tall, dark policeman with the tongue-tangling name had first called her, then walked into her flower shop holding the ad in his hand, Erin had looked upon it as nothing short of a miracle. But then, she was carrying a miracle inside of her, so she figured that in itself gave her the inside track on receiving another.

Sergeant Augustus Tripopulous had politely asked her if she'd placed the ad. When she had replied, mystified, that she had, the sergeant told her about the mugging victim he'd brought into the station house some five months earlier. And then he'd brought her here, to his sister's restaurant.

But not before Erin had gotten his uniform shirt wet with tears of utter relief.

Gus didn't even have to tell her about the St. Christopher's medallion around the victim's neck. He barely had to get into his story before Erin was certain that he had found Brady. In her heart, she just knew it. Or maybe if she believed enough, it would happen.

He'd cautioned her not to get her hopes up too high, but after all these bleak months of not knowing, Erin clung to that dizzying hope like a shipwreck survivor to a branch of driftwood that had passed within reach. She refused to even entertain the possibility that it wasn't her Brady.

Stopping only to collect the album of photographs Gus suggested she bring, she had left with him immediately. Somehow, even immediately seemed slow after waiting all this time.

It was only as she entered the restaurant that her nerves suddenly took over, threatening to undo the last threads of her composure. The aroma of Greek cuisine in Aphrodite's swirled all around her. Normally, that would have been enough to nudge her healthy appetite into second gear. But this afternoon, she moved like someone in a trance as Gus led her to a booth.

What if it wasn't him, after all?

Erin didn't think she could stand it if she was disappointed again.

He knew his name, but only his first name and that only because the policeman who had found him that hollow August evening he'd marked as the first day of the rest of his life had noticed the St. Christopher's medal around his neck.

"To Brady. Love, Erin."

That was all it said. The inscription was faded, rubbed smooth against his skin by the passing of days. That meant he'd had it for a while. The medallion was the only clue to the man he had been and the life he had had. The life he no longer remembered, thanks to a blow to his head. The scar had formed just below his hairline.

Brady didn't even know how he had gotten the injury, but given the condition Gus had found him in, a safe guess was that he had been mugged. The slight tan line on his left wrist and right ring finger showed that the mugger had not only made off with Brady's wallet, but his watch and ring, as well.

He'd made off with a great deal more than that, Brady thought in frustration as he piled the dishes from the rear table onto a tray. The man had made off with his identity.

For five months, Brady had lived in a vacuum, stepping out into each day enshrouded in a fog.

Tray in hand, Brady turned and saw Gus entering the restaurant. He was ushering in a very pregnant-looking redhead. Moving with the ease of someone in his second home, Gus walked toward table five. He had his hand on the redhead's arm. Brady noted that she wasn't looking where she was going. Instead, the woman was looking intently in his direction.

She was probably hungry, he mused, especially given her condition. He hoped she wasn't in the mood for the specialty of the house. They were all out of that. The lunch crowd had been particularly heavy this afternoon, but Brady didn't mind the hectic pace. He liked keeping busy. And with each person who entered Aphrodite's, Brady figured that his chances increased of seeing someone he might have once known. He hoped that when that happened, it would jar his dormant memory.

So far, nothing.

Table five was his station. Dropping off the tray of dishes on the water-slick conveyor belt that fed into the steam room, Brady took his pad and pencil out of his apron and made his way over to table five to see what Gus and his companion would have.

He was coming toward them. Erin's heart lurched and lodged in her mouth.

This was ridiculous. Her stomach was tied in a huge knot, barely allowing her to catch her breath. Why did she feel so nervous? It wasn't as if Brady was a stranger who she was meeting for the first time. He'd just acted like a stranger, dropping out of her life.

Out of everyone's life, she amended. But that was something she hadn't discovered until three weeks after the fact. She had only her own stubborn pride to blame for that. It was that same stubborn pride that had prevented her from going to Brady's apartment or his place of work, looking for him, until the trail was completely cold. No one knew where he was, or what had happened to him. All anyone knew was that he had gone to St. Louis on business—and disappeared.

Just as he'd threatened, Erin thought. His last words echoed again in her mind the way they did almost every day. *Maybe it would be better all around if I just stayed in St. Louis.* And then the door had slammed, cutting him out of her life. She'd had no way of knowing then for how long.

There was no family to turn to when he had disappeared. Brady didn't have any. And there were no clues to go on except that Brady Lockwood wasn't the kind of person who would just disappear without a word, even in the heat of anger.

Certainly there were no clues in his apartment to his sudden vanishing act. The only things missing were his suitcase and the few items he had packed for his trip. Everything within the modest one-bedroom home looked as if it were waiting for him to return.

Just the way she was.

The policeman in St. Louis who had taken down her statement when she'd finally flown there and reported Brady missing had looked at her with a kindly, knowing expression. She knew what he thought. That Brady had decided a pregnant girlfriend was more than he wanted to commit to and had very conveniently vanished. Though his words had been couched in gentle euphemisms, the policeman had suggested as much. After all, it wasn't that unusual an occurrence.

Indignantly, Erin had informed the officer that Brady hadn't known anything about her condition when he'd disappeared. She was sorry she had even mentioned that fact in her statement. At three months, she still hadn't looked pregnant.

The simple fact of the matter was that they'd had an argument, a heated one, and Brady had gone out, leaving her Bedford condo to cool off. Angry, stung and in a dilemma because the argument had been about having children, she hadn't bothered to ask Brady if he was coming back that evening. Instead, she had turned her back on him and for once had maintained her silence.

Over and over again in the next five months she'd upbraided herself for that.

Why hadn't she asked? Why hadn't she gone after him? Because she had been too damn stubborn, that was why. And now she was paying for it. Dearly.

Initially, when Brady hadn't returned, she'd assumed he had just gone on with his trip the next day. When he didn't call her, the way he normally did when he was away, she thought he was still angry. It was unlike him, and it worried her.

Brady didn't call while he was away, nor did he call her when he supposedly returned two weeks later. She had alternated between being upset and angry. Erin had thought the same thing that the questioning policeman had. That Brady had decided their relationship and her mercurial temper were not worth the trouble.

He had no way of knowing that her temper was on a roller-coaster ride because her hormones had gone out of whack, adjusting to her new condition.

She hadn't wanted to believe he'd just dumped her without a word, but everything had pointed to that. It was only after she finally broke down and called him at work that she'd learned they hadn't heard from him since he left for his trip. She had become really alarmed and had contacted the police in St. Louis.

So now, here she sat in a restaurant opposite a policeman who claimed he had found Brady wandering the streets, her nerves playing havoc with her as she watched the man she loved coming toward her without an iota of recognition in his eyes.

Erin sipped water from an amber glass to soothe the dryness in her throat. She could have drank a river, and it wouldn't have helped.

Though she prayed it was Brady, until this very moment, Erin couldn't quite get herself to believe the policeman's story about finding a mugging victim not far from where she lived. For one thing, muggings in her neighborhood were basically unheard of. Bedford was a peaceful city where people could walk the streets at night in safety. For another, the whole story about an amnesiac seemed like something that would happen in the pages of a book or in the movie of the week, not in her life.

Of course, if Brady had had amnesia, it would explain a great deal. He hadn't just left her of his own free will. She took solace in that.

And she needed solace right now because the look in Brady's blue eyes told her that this kind of thing didn't just happen on TV. It was happening to her.

"Hi, Gus, how's it going?"

The smile on Brady's face was one of warmth for the man he considered his partial savior. Gus had reached out to him at a time when he'd desperately needed to make contact with someone. When he had come to in that alley, everything about his life had been a complete blank.

For the most part, it still was. Brady knew, without knowing how, that he liked the color blue. But very little else had returned to him. At an age when men were getting to know people around them with more insight, fostering relationships with women who were in tune with their own likes and dislikes, Brady was stumbling around in the dark, trying to get to know himself.

"I'm fine, Brady," Gus answered carefully. "And I'll have the usual. How about you, Erin?"

The woman named Erin looked at Brady with a strange expression on her face. It was so pained and confused, it prompted him to ask, "Is something wrong, miss? I mean ma'am," he quickly amended in deference to her condition.

Yes, everything. Oh God, it's true. It was all true. Everything the policeman had told her was true.

Still, she hoped the sound of her voice would shatter that polite, distant look in Brady's eyes. "Brady?"

The woman's voice was light, reminding him of chimes swaying in the summer breeze. Where had that come from, he wondered suddenly, clinging to the snippet of a memory. He remembered chimes. Whose chimes? His? His family's? Damn. It was so frustrating, reaching out and trying to grasp something, only to have it turn into air in his hand.

Brady turned his attention back to the woman at the table. She knew his name. Did she know him? Or had Gus told her about finding him?

"Yes?"

There was no familiar note in his voice. He might as well have been talking to a stranger. Erin bit her lip. Brady's memory was really gone. It wasn't an act. The Brady she knew couldn't have put on a performance to save his life. What you saw was what you got.

She tried again, silently praying for yet another miracle. *Just one more, please.* "Brady, don't you know me?"

He wanted to. Oh, God, he wanted to know someone, something, a link to take him out of this vapid world he found himself so lost in.

But she didn't look familiar, although the scent she wore tickled something very, very far away, something he couldn't quite catch hold of.

Brady shook his head slowly. "No, I'm sorry, but I don't."

Erin covered her mouth and took a deep breath. Gus had warned her when he'd told her about Brady's condition that it wasn't going to be easy. That was why he had suggested she bring the photo album with her.

She placed her hand on top of it now, as if it could somehow act as a talisman. She'd found Brady. Now she needed to have him find her.

Confused, struggling with frustration, Brady looked at Gus for some sort of clarification.

Gus nodded his head. He gestured to the space beside him in the booth. "Why don't you sit down and join us?" After a moment's pause, Brady did. "I think we finally might have a last name for you, Brady."

Brady looked from the man who was his friend to the woman whose green eyes shimmered with a coating of tears. Eagerness nipped at him. "What is it?"

"Lockwood," Erin whispered, afraid that her voice would break if she spoke any louder. "Your name is Brady Lockwood."

He listened and played the name over in his mind. It didn't mean anything to him. A man's name should mean something, he thought, aggravated. It was his connection to the future, to the past. To immortality. But the name Brady Lockwood didn't mean anything to him.

The redhead Gus had called Erin was looking at him so hopefully, Brady almost felt as if he should be comforting her instead of inwardly railing against his misty prison.

Brady sighed. "I'm sorry. It just doesn't sound familiar."

Erin rose, bumping against the table with her rounded belly, filled to capacity with his child. Before Brady could prevent her, she leaned over and hooked her finger onto his chain. She pulled it out until the gold medallion lay exposed against the blue background of his shirt. Her trembling fingers surrounded it. Turning it over, she held it in the palm of her hand.

"I'm Erin," she said insistently. "Erin."

Tears filled her throat. This was almost as bad as finding him dead. Because everything he had been, everything they had had between them, was almost as good as dead. Erin turned the medallion around to the inscription, as if that would give validity to her words, to her existence.

"The Erin on the back of your St. Christopher's medal. You *have* to know me. I gave you that medallion two Christmases ago." It had been their first Christmas together. They'd made love for the first time that night. Her eyes pleaded with him. "Don't you remember?"

"Erin." He repeated the name as if it was a mantra, a key. But it opened nothing. "No," Brady replied. "I don't." She had no idea how sorry he was that he didn't, Brady thought.

Gus rose and placed his hand gently but firmly on Erin's shoulder. Her eyes shifted to him and he could feel his own heart wrenching within his chest at the misery he saw there.

"Why don't you sit down?" he said softly. In response, she sank onto her seat as if her legs had crumpled beneath her.

Brady sat in the booth, looking at Erin, waiting for the memories to come. Why didn't they? A man should remember a woman with skin of ivory, with hair like sunset and eyes that shimmered like clover growing wild in the field.

But he didn't. His mind was empty. He wondered if she had made a mistake, after all.

Very gently, Gus pushed the photo album to the center of the table. "Why don't you show him some of the photographs?" he suggested. He smiled encouragingly at Erin.

The album. That would do it, she thought, grasping at the straw. That would make Brady remember. She'd always insisted on bringing her camera along with them, commemorating anything they did with a slew of photographs. Brady used to groan every time he saw her raise it to her eye. She hadn't taken a photograph since he had left her life.

Quickly, she opened the well-worn book that she'd pored over all these months alone in her empty home. Fumbling, she flipped through pages, searching for something that would really jar his memory.

"Here," she cried, stabbing her finger at a photograph of Brady standing in front of the Christmas tree he had helped her select and decorate. It was a sorry-looking tree whose branches had drooped even as they brought it into her house. But she had said it needed love, and he had laughed at her, calling her hopelessly illogical. "Look at this one. I took this the Christmas I gave you the medallion."

Erin searched Brady's face and saw that the photograph and the memory depicted within meant nothing to him. He recognized himself and nothing more. Unease mounted as she flipped to another page.

"And here." She found another photograph she knew, hoped, prayed he would recall. "We went to San Francisco that long weekend you finally took off from work."

Someone else had obviously taken the photograph, he thought, looking at it for a long time. She was slim then. Her arms hooked through his, she was laughing as they sat on the side of a trolley.

He remembered a trolley, he realized. But had he seen it in another photograph, or did the memory actually come from the trip she said they had taken together?

Brady looked at her. What she had said interested him more than the photographs at his fingertips. "Work? What do I do?"

Though he was grateful for the job Demi had given him, in his heart Brady believed that in his other life he had worked with his mind and not his hands.

The question sounded strange, coming from him. His job—no, his career, she amended—had always been so very important to him.

"You're a physicist."

"Physicist." Brady rolled the word around on his tongue. It seemed to fit, through it evoked no flavors, no thoughts. He glanced at another photograph on the page. Nothing. It might as well have been taken of someone else. "Do I like it? Being a physicist, I mean."

For the first time, she smiled and laughed softly at the irony of the question.

"Like it? You live and breathe work. Or did." It would always feel as if she had to move heaven and earth to get Brady to take a little time off, or, at the very least, not work extra-long hours. Brady would always become immersed in his work, and then time would somehow seem to stop for him.

Just as it seemed to have stopped now, she thought.

Brady drew the album closer and began to page through it methodically, starting at the beginning and working his way to the end.

Just like Brady. She watched him in silence, afraid to form a thought, a prayer. Hoping. She had her fingers crossed without realizing it.

Finally, when he was finished, Brady closed the album and sat back. With a sigh, he moved the book across the table, pushing it toward Erin. He shook his head in response to the question in her eyes.

"Are we married?" he asked suddenly. Even as he did, he looked at her left hand. It was bare.

Erin shook her head slowly. But they were going to be, she remembered with a bittersweet pang. It was one of those understandings that went without saying. But how could she put that into words for this stranger with Brady's face?

"No."

But she was something to him, Brady decided. There were too many photographs for there not to have been some sort of a connection between them. "Divorced?"

That was the kind of question Brady would ask, she thought, a sad smile twisting her lips. He was in there somewhere. She just had to find a way to set him free. "No, we never got that far."

Her phrasing intrigued him. His eyes shifted to the swell of her abdomen.

He didn't have to form the words. Erin raised her chin without realizing it.

"Yes," she answered, telling him what she couldn't bring herself to tell him that day he'd walked out on her. That she was carrying his child—and had been for the last eight months. "The baby is yours."

Her answer disturbed him. Then why hadn't he married her? Was he that kind of person? The type to selfishly abandon a woman who was pregnant with his child? The discovery left a bad taste in his mouth.

What other things were lurking in his past that would make him uncomfortable with himself? For the first time, Brady wondered if perhaps his accident had been for the best, after all. It amounted to a second chance. A way to leave off the old life and start fresh with a new one.

But he couldn't do that if there were ends left to be tied. And she was very obviously one of those.

"And I walked out on you?"

He didn't remember, she thought. None of it. And certainly not the heated words they had exchanged that had left her so numb and generated the horrid feeling in the pit of her stomach that had made her nauseated. Sadness washed over her, bleaching her very bones.

She watched Brady's eyes as she spoke, slowly, deliberately, hoping that her words would stir something within him.

"No, you walked out on a...discussion we were having. You went to cool off. You just never came back.'' Erin pressed her lips together and swallowed. She wasn't getting through to him. But it didn't matter, not right now. He was alive and that was all that counted. She could take it from here. ''Until now.''

2

There were so many questions scrambling over one another in Erin's mind, vying for prominence, all demanding answers. But above them all was one that echoed over and over again in her brain.

Why don't you know me, Brady? You said I was the only thing in your life that ever mattered to you besides your work. And you forgot us both.

Confronted with the fathomless look in Brady's eyes, Erin felt overwhelmed. She clenched her hands in her lap, struggling to regain control. This was no time to fall apart. She was going to have to serve as Brady's key to the past. She couldn't unlock anything for him if she allowed herself to indulge in self-pity. It was Brady who mattered right now, not her hurt feelings or anything else. Just Brady.

"There's just so much I have to ask you," Erin began, trying to organize the questions that were slamming into one another like untrained skaters on the ice for the first time. Where were his clothes? He'd had a suitcase with him when he disappeared. Was that gone? Did he remember anything? She chose the first question that popped up. "How did you happen to wind up working here?"

There were a great many questions he couldn't answer, at least this one he could. Brady's eyes shifted to the policeman beside her. He wasn't sure what he would have done without the man's support.

"Gus brought me. Demi gave me a job waiting tables to carry me over until my memory returned. I'm still waiting." A self-deprecating smile curved his generous mouth. "No pun intended."

"Demi?" Erin repeated.

She looked from the uniformed man at her side to Brady, her heart accelerating again, this time in alarm. Was there another woman in the picture now? Had the new Brady, the one who couldn't remember her or the life they had shared, found someone else in these last few months? The possibility had never occurred to Erin before.

"My sister," Gus explained quickly, noting the look of distress rising in Erin's eyes.

Leaning out of the booth, Gus beckoned to a raven-haired woman standing behind the cashier's desk. She approached them on long, shapely legs that made Erin's heart sink a little lower.

"This is my sister, Demitria Tripopulous," Gus introduced the woman to her. "Demi, this is Erin Collins, the woman who ran the ad that Grandmother read."

Demi smiled warmly as she shook Erin's hand. "Nice to meet you. So?" She looked hopefully at her brother and then Brady, taking them both in in one long, sweeping glance. "Any luck?"

Gus shook his head. In his own way, he felt as disappointed about the outcome as the chief players were. "Not yet. The doctor said these things take time." Gus explained to Erin, "Some amnesia victims completely regain their memory within a few weeks of their loss. Others take years and still others just keep waiting. In general, it takes a few months."

"And some never recover," Brady added. He remembered how the words had sunk deeply into his soul when he first heard the doctor utter them. It felt as if he had been branded by a red-hot iron.

"And some do," Erin interjected. Erin had very little knowledge about amnesia, but she was well schooled in optimism, and that was something she had always tried to drum into Brady's head. If you were optimistic, the time you spent waiting was always upbeat. She intended to remain upbeat now. After all, she'd found him, hadn't she?

Brady looked at Erin sharply as a feeling of déjà vu whispered through him. But it had no substance, no breadth. He couldn't grasp it, couldn't examine it any further. And then it was gone. Frustration beat through him as it did a hundred times a day. He sighed and shrugged in response to her words.

"I think," Demi said brightly, "in honor of Brady learning his last name, a celebration is in order. What'll you have?" she asked Erin. "On the house," she added when Erin said nothing.

Food was the last thing on her mind right now. Erin held the photo album, pressing it against her chest. Somehow, just holding the visual evidence of their life together comforted her. She offered an apologetic smile to Gus's sister.

"I'm afraid I'm not hungry right now." She looked around the restaurant. The lunch crowd had thinned out, but Aphrodite's was still far from empty. "Is there somewhere private where Brady and I can talk?" she asked Demi.

Anticipation and apprehension vied for space within him. As much as he wanted to know who he was, he wasn't prepared to face it in a busy restaurant with onlookers. Something told him he was a private person.

Brady rose from the table. "My shift's not over yet."

"Wow." Demi shook her head in bemused surprise. "I wish everyone who worked here was as dedicated as you are."

He didn't see it as dedication particularly, just living up to an obligation. She paid him to work, not to sit and talk. As eager as he was to find out who he was, he realized that it wasn't going to happen with a bolt of lightning striking him.

Demi tugged on his apron strings. The apron loosened and she pulled it away from him. "Yes, it is." He looked at her questioningly. "Your shift is over," she emphasized.

Brady surprised them all by taking the apron from her hands. He needed a routine to hang on to. However small, he needed some sort of structure in his life so that he could build from there.

"No, not yet," he told Demi quietly.

Though she felt frustrated by his actions, Erin was heartened at the same time. That much was still Brady, Erin thought, that stubborn, methodical way that he approached everything he did.

Gathering the album and her purse, Erin struggled out of the booth's confinement. Freed, she rose to her feet and turned toward Brady. It was hard standing so close to him and not throwing her arms around his neck, not holding him close and sobbing her relief, but she contained herself. She didn't want to frighten him away. In a way, she realized, this was almost like the beginning of their relationship. She had fallen in love with him the moment she'd seen him. It had taken her a year before she convinced him that he felt the same way.

"All right, why don't you come home—to my house," she corrected. "When you're through working?"

Maybe that was a better idea, anyway. The three months before he had vanished, he had practically lived at her house. She might not be able to trigger his memory, but maybe something there would. At least she could hope. She could *always* hope.

Brady looked at her, trying to remember. He shook his head. "I don't know—"

Anticipating his words, Erin stopped Brady with a wave of her hand before he finished. "Could I have your pad and pencil, please?"

He gave it to her wordlessly and then watched as Erin tore off a sheet. Flipping it over to the blank side, she wrote down her address for him.

"Here." Erin handed the paper to him. "This is where I live."

It felt so strange having to tell him her address. Brady had helped her choose her condo. She'd consulted with him on all the new furnishings, secretly knowing that one day this would be where they would live. In her own haphazard approach to life, Erin had planned it all out.

She fought back a fresh onslaught of emotion. They'd made her home together, and now he didn't even know where that had been.

Brady looked down at the address, then raised his eyes to hers. "I'm not that familiar with the area."

Gus moved next to Brady and glanced at the paper in his hand. "It's where I found you." Brady didn't have a driver's license yet, nor did he have a car at his disposal. Demi had given him a place to stay behind the kitchen, so there was no urgent need to get a license. It occurred to Gus that he didn't even know if Brady remembered *how* to drive. "Look, why don't I come by here later and run you up there myself?"

Brady nodded, grateful for the help. He folded the piece of paper and tucked it into his shirt pocket. "Seven o'clock all right with you?" he asked Erin.

Erin nodded, blinking back tears. She wanted to cry out, "No, come home with me now. I've been through hell and back in the last five months. I don't want to wait another five hours." She didn't. Instead, she struggled to control her emotions. He was so formal, so polite. Just as when they'd met. Back to square one. But she had won him over once, and she would do it again.

She had to.

She pressed her lips together before answering. "Seven is fine with me."

Despite all her best efforts, one of the tears she was trying so valiantly to hold back slid down her cheek.

The sight of it saddened Brady, stirring him. Stirring something.

"Um, hey, don't." He had no idea what prompted him, but he reached out and gently wiped away the tear from her cheek with his thumb. Maybe it was because she looked so sad. Or maybe it was because he knew that he was responsible for its existence.

Touching her cheek prodded something in the recesses of his mind. But the next moment, it was gone, fading as if it had never been. It was like a two-step, he thought. One step forward, one step back. When would he finally be on his way forward?

"Maybe I'll remember soon." He dug into his pocket and handed her his handkerchief.

Erin sniffed as she accepted it. That was so like him, she thought. He was the only man she'd ever known who actually carried a handkerchief.

She shook her head, wanting only to leave him with a positive impression. "No, it's not that." She wiped her eyes, silently forbidding herself any more tears. "It's just that I'm so glad you're alive."

People around them were staring, she realized. Not that it really mattered to her. But it always had to Brady. He never liked attracting attention. When he had held her hand in public, she had thought of it as a major event.

Erin blew out a breath and handed the handkerchief back to Brady. She mustered the cheeriest voice she could. "I'll see you at seven."

Brady nodded. He was still standing in the same spot, watching her as she walked out of the restaurant with Gus holding her arm.

Gus opened the front door and held it for her. He had to be getting back. This was his lunch hour. He looked down at the small woman beside him. "Do you want to go home?"

That was the last place she wanted to go. She needed time to pull herself together, and she always did it best surrounded by people.

Erin shook her head in response, holding on to her album tightly. "Brady's not the only one who has work to do. I can't just leave Terry to handle everything," she said, referring to her assistant.

Gus wasn't convinced that was the best thing for her right now. He looked pointedly at her abdomen. On the way to the restaurant, she had told him that she was eight months pregnant.

"You've had a shock," Gus began.

Erin squared her shoulders. She liked to proudly say that she was from sturdy, peasant stock. At times, that really helped.

"I've been living a shock for the last five months, Gus. This is a relief." She glanced back toward the restaurant as she thought of the blank look in Brady's eyes when he'd first looked at her. "Sort of," she amended quietly.

She sat down in Gus's squad car and drew the seat belt over herself, struggling to get the metal clip into the slot. These days, it was always a battle for leverage, she mused.

She waited until Gus sat behind the wheel before continuing, "Do you really think he'll get his memory back? I mean, eventually?" She could hang on if she just felt that someday Brady would look at her the way he used to.

Gus attempted to sound positive. "The doctor said it was hopeful."

The doctor had also said a great many other things that he wasn't about to go into now with this woman. She'd had enough of a shock for one day, no matter what she said to the contrary. Besides, there was no reason not to be optimistic about the outcome. Look at the odds against his ever having seen that ad she had run. Anything was possible.

The doctor. She hadn't thought to ask about that before. Erin turned in her seat. The belt was strangling her, so she adjusted it as best she could. "*You* took him to see a doctor?"

Gus waited for a truck to pass before he turned onto the main drag. "Yes."

He said it as if it wasn't an unusual thing. She thought of the original policeman she had spoken with in St. Louis. The one who had looked so sympathetic and then never contacted her again. "Isn't that a little above and beyond the call of duty?"

Gus shrugged as he changed lanes. He glanced in her direction and smiled. "No, not really. It's pretty standard procedure, actually."

"But finding him a job and a place to stay aren't," she guessed.

His grin turned a bit sheepish around the edges. "I kind of get involved in my work."

And didn't that sound familiar? Erin settled against her seat and sighed. "So does Brady. So *did* Brady." Should she talk about him in the past tense, or the present? she wondered. Now that he was found, she supposed it should be in the present, but in a way, he was still missing, at least to her.

Erin rolled down the window a little. Her mind dashed about, clutching at bits and pieces of fragmented thoughts. He was alive. Brady was alive. She closed her eyes, letting the breeze caress her face. Somehow, life was going to get back to normal. It just had to.

She thought of the way Brady had looked when she told him what he did for a living. It coaxed a smile from her. "Boy, are they going to be happy at the lab to see him."

Gus arched an eyebrow. "You mean, his job is still waiting for him after all these months?"

She had called Edmond Labs just last week, to see if anyone had heard anything. Mr. Waverly was still concerned about the disappearance of one of his best scientists. He'd reassured her that Brady was still needed. It had almost made her cry again.

"They think very highly of him there. Brady has a very sharp mind." Erin stared straight ahead at the early-afternoon traffic as Gus drove to Newport Beach and her shop. "It's just sleeping right now."

And it was her job to wake it up, Erin thought. She only hoped she was equal to it.

"He's going to be all right, Erin."

"I know that." Erin turned to look at him. "I want to thank you for everything that you've done for Brady. I know you didn't have to."

Gus shrugged. He hadn't been able to bring himself to think of the lost man as just another case and file him away. "It wasn't all that much. Demi thinks he's a very hard worker."

"Yes, yes, he is. He always was." She paused, hesitating. Maybe she was out of place asking, but she had to. "Your sister isn't...I mean, she's not..." Her voice trailed off.

Gus seemed to read her thoughts. "No, she isn't interested in Brady." He grinned then. "Demi's too busy telling the rest of us how to live our lives."

"Rest?" Erin asked, curious.

"Me and an assorted number of cousins. Eventually, she'll make someone a great wife." As long as that man could hold his own against a steamroller. "But it won't be Brady."

Erin relaxed. That was nice to hear. "Yes, I'm sure she will."

"And he doesn't remember anything?" Nicole Logan's incredulous voice drifted through the small shop, mingling with a profusion of flowers that lined the shelf on the back wall.

She exchanged glances with her sister, Marlene. Both women had met Erin through their obstetrician and comprised in part what Dr. Sheila Pollack fondly referred to as her Baby of the Month Club. Marlene had given birth to her son in December, while Nicole rang in the new year with twins. With approximately a month to go, that left February to Erin.

The two women had walked through the door of Flowers by Erin exactly two minutes before Erin had returned from the restaurant. Wrapped up in their own budding wedding plans, it had taken a moment for the agitated look on Erin's face to register with the sisters. When it did, they rapidly fired questions at her before Erin even had a chance to put away her purse. They were joined by Terry. All three women knew about Brady and his sudden disappearance. Everyone who knew Erin did.

Erin shook her head in answer to Nicole's original question. "No, nothing." But she was undaunted. During the ride home, she had decided that Brady was going to get his memory back. It was only a matter of time. Erin looked at the three stunned faces around her. "But it's only temporary," she added, as much for their sake as her own. She smiled at Marlene. "It was the ad you suggested that did it. I ran an ad in the personals column," she clarified when Marlene didn't seem to remember. "Both in St. Louis and here." She had wanted to leave no stone unturned. "Lucky for me Gus's grandmother saw it. She brought his attention to it, saying that it was an odd coincidence that the names in the ad were the same as on St. Christopher's medal."

Erin was definitely going too fast for her. "Gus?" Marlene asked. She glanced at Nicole, but her sister only shrugged. Nicole was as lost as she was.

"St. Christopher's medal?" Nicole echoed. "Whose St. Christopher's medal?"

Erin took a deep breath and began again. She had a habit of talking faster than most people could listen. Brady used to tease her that she talked enough for both of them combined, so he didn't have to talk at all. She had always countered that it was his excuse for getting out of conversations.

"Gus is the policeman who found Brady." She was getting ahead of herself again. "Brady was mugged when he left my house that night. He never made it to St. Louis.''

At least she supposed he hadn't, even though his flight ticket had been used. Suffering from amnesia, he wouldn't have been able to find his way back. The only thing she knew for a fact was that his car was missing, his ticket had been used and he never stayed in the hotel room that had been reserved for him.

''Oh, how awful for him. For you,'' Marlene sympathized. She thought of how she would feel if it had been Sullivan who had been mugged. She couldn't even begin to put the feelings into words, even in her own mind.

''He's all right now,'' Erin assured her. *Thank God.* ''Anyway, his wallet had been stolen, and he didn't have any identification on him except for the medallion I gave him.'' She came to a skidding halt in her own narrative. ''I guess whoever mugged him must have missed that, thank goodness. Anyway, that's how they knew his name,'' she explained. ''At least his first name. And mine. So, when Gus—that's the policeman,'' she added in case they had missed that, ''told his grandmother about finding Brady, she remembered the details. She's ninety years old, he said, but remembers everything as if it happened yesterday.'' Erin stopped abruptly, biting her lower lip. ''Unlike Brady.''

Nicole was still trying to assimilate the details. ''And he really doesn't know you?''

Erin ran her hands along her arms, staving off the cold that came from within. "No."

Marlene placed her arm around Erin and drew her closer. Her heart went out to the younger woman. "What are you going to do?"

Erin didn't want sympathy. She was going to get through this. There was no doubt in her mind. Just as there hadn't been that somehow, some way, Brady would return to her. And he had. In a manner of speaking.

"Work at it until he knows me. I'm going to reintroduce him to everything and everyone he's ever known." Very gently, she extricated herself from Marlene. "Somewhere is the trigger that'll set it all off. I just have to find it." She sighed as she went around to the other side of the counter. "I wish I had Brady to help me. He was always good at things like this." The irony of it all struck her and she smiled to herself.

Erin looked up at the women, suddenly realizing that she had allowed herself to go on at length. "But you didn't come here to hear me talk about my life."

"In part," Marlene corrected.

"And the other part?" Erin coaxed. She could see by the look in her friend's eyes that something was definitely up.

"The other part is that we're going to need flowers." Nicole grinned. She looked at Marlene, her pleasure growing enough to burst. "Lots of flowers."

"Music to my ears," Erin agreed. She cocked her head. "What's the occasion?" If she was any judge, something told her she already knew.

"A wedding," Marlene said.

"Two," Nicole added.

Erin looked from one woman to the other. She had known that both were interested in men when they'd talked at the Christmas party Dr. Pollack had thrown. She hadn't expected anything to come to fruition so quickly, though. "When?"

"Next week," Marlene said.

"I know it's hopelessly sentimental," Marlene confessed, "but I always wanted something like this."

Nicole turned to look at her sister in surprise. "You never told me that."

"Because you were always such a cynic. I was afraid you'd laugh at me." Nicole had always been the rebel, while Marlene had been the dependable one. "And then you ran off with Craig, so I just assumed that was the end of it."

But life—thank God, Marlene thought—had other, better plans for both of them.

Erin concentrated on her friends. If she allowed her thoughts to turn to Brady, she wouldn't be able to do anything else but think of him.

"Are you marrying the tax lawyer you told me about?" she asked Nicole. "The one who was so neighborly all the time?"

Nicole smiled, remembering how she had complained about that. Life with her late husband had taught her to be cautious of any overt gestures of friendship. But Dennis had managed to break down her barriers. "Yes, but he's not a tax lawyer. He turned out to be a Justice Department investigator."

Erin looked at Nicole in surprise. "What was he investigating?"

"Me."

At the time, Nicole had been horrified to discover the duplicity. But everything had turned out all right, and Dennis had saved her life in the bargain.

Erin placed her hand to her forehead. It wasn't often that she was on the receiving end of confusion. "I think I'm getting a headache here. Would you mind running that by me again?"

It was a story to be told over a hot cup of coffee on a cold, lazy winter afternoon. Right now, Erin was living through her own crisis. "Maybe this isn't the right time to explain it all," Marlene suggested. "If you want us to come back another time—"

Erin hurried around the counter, hooking a hand through each of the two women's arms. "No, no, believe me, I need to keep busy." She looked from one to the other. "Otherwise, all I'll think about is tonight."

Nicole arched an eyebrow. "Tonight?"

Erin felt her palms growing damp just at the thought. "Gus is bringing Brady by my house tonight at seven. I was hoping that familiar surroundings might get him to start piecing things together." She blew out a breath, blocking out the negative thoughts that were trying to break through. ''Okay, so when's the wedding? I mean, weddings,'' she corrected. ''And what kind of flowers will you be wanting?''

''We're having the weddings at my house a week Sunday.'' Marlene took out her notepad. She had everything written out, down to the last detail.

Erin grinned. ''Boy, when you get going, you certainly don't waste any time.''

''You're invited, of course,'' Nicole told her.

''Well, in that case, you get a break on the price.'' Erin winked. She took Marlene's list and began making notes in the margin.

Erin paced her living room, her hand resting nervously on her stomach. As she passed by the mantel, she glanced at the clock. She'd been checking the time since she'd arrived home at six. In the last half hour, she'd looked at the clock so many times, she was surprised that she hadn't worn the face away.

Or worn a path in the rug between the sofa and the door. Each time she thought she heard a car pass, she hurried to the peephole to look out. But no one appeared on her doorstep. As the minutes ticked away, her agitation intensified.

Turning away from the door again, she looked down at her stomach. ''I don't want you taking note of this, Jamie.'' Since the moment she discovered that she was pregnant, she had addressed the baby as Jamie. It was one of those names that could fit either sex, and more important, it was Brady's middle name and she loved it. "I know I'm acting like a kid waiting for her first date to show up, but there's a reason for that. In a way, this *is* my first date with him."

She moved the curtain aside and looked out. There was no one on the street. Erin let the curtain drop. This anxiousness was reminiscent of so many other evenings, when she had waited for him to return, only to go to bed alone. At least she knew he was coming tonight.

"Oh, God, we have to make him remember. We just have to." She cupped her hand around her belly again. "Not because he's your dad. I don't want him coming back to us out of a sense of obligation. I want him coming back to us because he wants to. Because he loves us. Because he remembers that he loves us. I mean, me." She smiled ruefully. "He didn't even know anything about you when he left."

Erin winced as the baby kicked hard.

"I know, I know. I should have told him about you, but I was afraid." She sighed. "I was afraid to tell him he was going to be a father while he was going on about how children shouldn't be brought into a world like ours. That's how we got into that argument."

She shivered as she thought of the heated words that had passed between them. Words she hadn't meant to say. Words she had wanted to take back. She tended to become very emotional where her feelings were concerned.

"And I said some things I shouldn't have, and so did he..." She was babbling. Nerves. "But you heard all that, didn't you?"

She looked at the clock. It was exactly seven. Where was he? she wondered.

Erin raised her head as she heard the sound of a car approaching. She took a deep cleansing breath and then released it. It didn't help. She still felt as nervous as a cat that had been dropped in the middle of a dog pound.

The next minute, the doorbell rang. Her heart jumped. He was here.

Finally.

Erin pressed her hand against her stomach once more. "Here goes nothing," she whispered to her baby. "And just maybe everything."

3

Gus turned to Brady a moment before he rang Erin's doorbell.

"Nervous?"

"Yes." Brady nodded, staring at the door. Nothing. He remembered nothing.

Even his hands were perspiring. He wanted so much to remember, and he was so afraid that he never would.

Gus rested a hand on Brady's shoulder in a gesture of camaraderie. "I would be, too, if I were in your place." Gus couldn't begin to imagine what it had to be like, coming to and not knowing anything about himself. Not remembering Demi or his life. He tried to commiserate. "I suppose it's a little like free falling out of an airplane without seeing the ground."

Brady considered the comparison for a minute. He was always very careful when he spoke, as if he had to examine every word before it was freed. After a moment, he decided Gus's analysis was as good an analogy of his situation as any.

"Something like that." He wrapped his hand around the doorknob, wanting to feel something, a touch of familiarity. Anything. "I don't know if the ground is going to rush up and flatten me, or cradle me."

The smile on Gus's face was encouraging. "I guess that all depends if the chute opens."

"Yeah." Brady let out a breath as he braced himself to leap from the hypothetical airplane. "All right, let's find out if the chute opens. Go ahead, ring the doorbell."

Gus did. After only a second, the door swung open. Erin was standing there, breathless even though she'd been only a few steps away.

She looks afraid, too, Brady thought. *Beneath that wide smile, she looks afraid. Well, that makes two of us.* Somehow, the knowledge made him feel just a little better.

Brady nodded at her, his feet rooted to the welcome mat. "Hi."

"Hi." After a beat, she realized that Gus was standing beside him. Erin nodded at Gus as she stepped back from the doorway. "Come on in."

She was holding on to the doorknob so hard, she thought her fingerprints would be permanently sealed into the brass. This felt so awkward. Erin fought off a fresh wave of despair. She shouldn't have to be inviting Brady into a place that had been as much of a home to him as his apartment. More so.

Striving to be cheerful, Erin closed the door behind them. Gus looked different in civilian clothes. Less authoritative, she supposed. Brady was still wearing the same shirt he'd had on in the restaurant. Blue. His favorite color. She wondered if he knew that.

She'd practiced what she was going to say when Brady arrived. Over and over again in the car and then here, she had formed perfect sentences. Right now, she couldn't remember any of them. For once in her life, she was at a loss for what to say.

Desperate, she turned toward Gus. "Thanks for bringing him."

Gus glanced around the room. It was a nice house, he decided. A hell of a lot nicer than his. But then, chaos suited him. He had a feeling from what Erin had told him and from what he'd observed himself that it wouldn't suit Brady.

Erin watched, holding her breath, as Brady moved through the living room. She could almost see his thoughts as they marched through his mind. He was carefully taking in his surroundings, as if he was cataloging them and placing them in order. He might not remember being a scientist, she thought with a subdued smile, but his mind did.

Brady stopped by the large, U-shaped sofa that dominated the room. The white leather appealed to him. He wasn't so sure about the painting that hung on the wall directly over it, though.

"You have a very nice place here," he finally said quietly.

Erin joined him in front of the sofa. She wanted to thread her arm through his, but refrained. One tiny step at a time, she told herself.

"You helped decorate it." She saw the way he was looking at the painting, as if he was trying to make a decision. Or as if he was trying to remember. Her heart skipped a beat. "We argued a lot about that painting." He raised an eyebrow as he turned toward her. The painting was a blend of warm colors that splashed into one another, depicting nothing. "I won."

He nodded. That made sense. The large reproduction didn't really look like something he might like.

At least, he didn't think so.

That was what made it so hard getting through each day, not knowing anything about himself, waiting for some sort of breakthrough to take place. Did he have secrets? Was he friendly or reclusive? It was all lost to him. He hated not knowing.

Most of all, he thought, glancing in Erin's direction, he hated not remembering her or the child she carried.

"It's colorful," he murmured.

Erin grabbed his hand, excitement telegraphing itself through her. Taken by surprise, Brady looked into her startled eyes for an explanation.

The words tangled on her tongue. "You said that." She swallowed, sorting out the phrases as her eyes darted to Gus and then back to Brady. "That's exactly what you said when you gave up trying to convince me not to buy it." Realizing that she was squeezing his hand, she released it, smiling ruefully. Hope danced through her on silver toe-shoes. "You always had a graceful way of conceding an argument." Until the last time, she corrected herself.

She looked at Gus, elation and eagerness shining in her eyes. Gus nodded his mute support, then asked, "Would you like me to stay?" He posed the question to Erin as well as Brady.

Emotionally, Erin knew that she could use the support. But this was Brady, she reminded herself. She needed to be alone with him, needed to go over intimate details that had been a part of their everyday lives. She couldn't do that with Gus here.

She shook her head. "No, thank you. I'm sure you have things to do, and we've already imposed enough on your kindness."

In her own way, she took charge, Gus mused. Just like his sister. What was it his father had called Demi? The iron butterfly, that was it. It seemed that the title fit more than one person.

Gus glanced at Brady, who nodded his agreement. "Then I'll be back later to pick you up," Gus promised.

Erin didn't want Brady leaving again so soon now that he was finally here. Maybe she was being unduly cautious, silly, even, but the last time he had left, he'd been gone for five months. She was afraid. Afraid of watching him walk out that door again.

Erin talked fast as she looked from one man to the other. "Maybe it would be better if Brady stayed the night. You know, wake up in a familiar place and all that.'' Her eyes darted back and forth, full of hope. And apprehension. ''There's a spare bedroom...'' It was crammed right now with Brady's possessions, things she had brought over from his apartment before the landlord could confiscate them. She'd paid the man part of Brady's last month's rent just to get them.

Brady barely nodded. It didn't seem right, staying with a woman he didn't know. Somehow, it didn't seem fair to her.

He exchanged glances with Gus, but couldn't read the other man's thoughts. ''We'll see.''

Gus glanced at his watch. ''I could be back in a couple of hours or so.'' He looked at Erin. ''That okay?''

It would have to be. She nodded.

Erin walked with Gus to the door, her legs shaky. He gave her a warm smile just before he left, but it didn't help assuage the queasy feeling in her stomach. When she shut the door behind him, it took a great deal of courage for her to turn around and see the look on Brady's face. The look that said he didn't know her.

''Would you like some coffee?'' Before he could answer, Erin continued quickly, ''You always took it black as midnight.''

He thought of the coffee he drank at the restaurant on his break. He'd instinctively taken it that way. ''All right.''

She turned to lead the way to the kitchen. She stopped when he didn't follow. Erin looked over her shoulder. "Why don't you come with me?"

Brady had always liked sitting in the kitchen. The kitchen, he had maintained, was the heart of a home. Not the bedroom, not the living room, but the kitchen, where he would always spread out his work, leaving little room to eat. Or sit in the wee hours of the morning, reading. How many times had she found him like that? Too many to remember. But he had to.

"All right."

Brady followed her through the living room, down a small hall adorned with framed photographs of people he didn't recognize. He paused before the last one, squinting as if that small action could awaken the memory.

"What is it?" she asked urgently. It was on the tip of her tongue to tell him who the young man was, but she bit it back.

"I don't know...." He shook his head. "I just thought...never mind. I don't know him."

"That was your father," she said quietly. "The little boy in the picture is you."

The murky curtain wouldn't lift.

"My father...?" He turned to her.

She second-guessed the question. "He died a few years ago. Your mother passed away when you were fifteen."

"Then I'm all alone?"

She shook her head. "No," she said with feeling. "You have me."

Erin stopped at the threshold, letting him enter the kitchen first. She watched his face as he looked around. His eyes met hers, and he shook his head.

"That's okay." She forced a cheery note into her voice. All he needed was time, she told herself. Erin crossed to the coffeemaker and began to pour coffee for both of them.

If she truly was part of his life, he probably had witnessed this scene a hundred times. Why didn't it look familiar to him? He'd been waiting all these months to meet someone from his past, and now that he finally had, nothing had changed except for the level of frustration. It was almost insurmountable.

"I've been trying to remember you all afternoon," he confessed as he watched her back. Brady saw her shoulders stiffen slightly in expectation.

Very carefully, she filtered the disappointment out of her voice. "No luck, huh?"

"No." The word came out on a sigh. "Although your perfume . . ."

He broke off. Erin turned around to face him, a coffee cup in each hand. "Yes?"

The one word was steeped in eagerness. The sound fairly surrounded him. He wished to God for both their sakes that he could say something positive to her.

"It smells familiar." But that could be for no other reason than someone's having had worn it once at the restaurant.

Erin set the cups on the table, moving one in front of him.

"It should." He raised a questioning eyebrow. "You gave it to me for my birthday. Two weeks before you disappeared."

He paused, thoughtful, as he sipped the dark brew she had placed before him. The hot, bitter liquid swirled down his throat and into his belly. Brady raised his eyes to hers. "Good."

"I know." She smiled. "You taught me how to make it." Erin drew her chair closer to his and sat down. "I used to tease you that you could eat your coffee with a knife and fork." Her smile was nostalgic, as if she were speaking of someone else. Remembering someone else, he thought. "You maintained that if coffee wasn't strong, what was the sense of drinking it?"

He watched the overhead fluorescent light shimmer on the inky surface in his coffee cup. There was love in her voice when she spoke of him. Had he been lovable?

He searched her face. "What am I like, Erin? As a person, what am I like?"

He wanted the answer without embellishments. She knew that tone in his voice even if he didn't. For once, she thought before launching into her reply.

"Well, you're good and kind." Her eyes shifted to his face. "A little stubborn sometimes, but that's a good thing—" Erin thought of their last argument with a pang. Looking back, it had been as much her fault as his. Maybe even more. But that didn't change what had happened afterward. If there had been no argument, they wouldn't be having this conversation. "Usually."

She might as well have been describing someone else, Brady thought. He set down his cup and put his face in his hands.

Startled, moved, eager to comfort, Erin placed her hand on his shoulder. "Don't," she implored. She couldn't stand to see him like this, so lost, so distant.

The pressure on his shoulder felt familiar, but then, one human being's touch was pretty much like another. It didn't make him remember her any more clearly. It didn't make him remember her at all.

When he looked up at her again, embarrassed for the momentary lapse, he saw the genuine concern in her eyes. It drew words from him that under different circumstances he would have kept to himself.

"You don't know what it's like, not knowing. Do I do this, do I do that? Do I like strawberries . . . ?"

She grinned, grasping the solid question. "Yes, you do. A great deal. And as for the rest, it'll come to you."

It has to, she prayed.

He didn't feel nearly as optimistic about his situation as Erin did. Or Gus, for that matter. The man had said the same words to him on more than one occasion. "It hasn't so far."

An overwhelming desire to somehow rip through the shroud that covered his brain and bring back the man she loved rippled through her. She had the will, but no weapons. Yet.

"Give it time, Brady. Until then, look at it as a big adventure." She knew she was reaching, but she had to say something. She'd glimpsed the despair in his eyes, and it tore at her. "There's a whole host of sensations to experience for the first time." Erin smiled at him. "Again."

He looked at her as if he was weighing her words. "You're an optimist, aren't you?"

At times, that had been a dirty word for him. She grinned. "Yup."

He thought for a moment. "I don't think I am." He said it as if it was a revelation. In a way, for him, it was.

"Not usually," she said in agreement. She wondered if he was remembering or guessing. "You're very pragmatic," she added in his defense.

Brady nodded slowly. That sounded right. What he had learned about himself in the last five months would point in that direction.

"Maybe you're right," he told her. "Maybe it will come back to me."

She reached across the table and covered his hand with her own.

"It will," she promised. "It will."

He looked down at her hand. There was something comforting about it. Something almost—but not quite—familiar, like a dream that was fading even as he desperately tried to remember it upon waking.

Brady sighed, disgusted. "This is like walking in a fog. Like evening in London." He looked at Erin sharply as soon as he had spoken the words. "How would I know that?"

Erin's heart quickened. A piece of his puzzle was falling into place. Haphazardly, but it was there. The grin on her face was wide.

"Because you *were* in London. Last spring," she added quickly. "The lab sent you to attend a huge conference." All the way to the airport, he had complained about having to make the presentation. "You didn't want to go." It had pleased her, when they parted, that he told her he was going to miss her. Brady didn't usually get sentimental. "You read a paper on the latest developments of laser optics." She saw the look in his eyes. A glimmer of a light dawning.

"You remember," she whispered. It was more of a statement than a question.

He nodded his head as if he was in a trance. "Something." He closed his eyes, trying to draw the fragments together so he could make sense of them. He felt her hand tightening on his. "Standing in front of people, reading." He opened his eyes. There wasn't any more. "It was awkward."

He was in there, all right. And every minute, he was closer to surfacing. It was going to be all right. She let out the breath she was holding.

"You hate presentations," she told him.

Yes, he did, he thought suddenly. He didn't like drawing attention to himself.

Expectantly, Brady looked around the kitchen again. But it didn't look any more familiar now than it had a few minutes ago. No lightning breakthrough, he thought. Just one tiny piecelet at a time. Piecelet? Where had that come from? It wasn't a word.

He saw her looking at him so hopefully. It only increased the frustration he felt.

"But if I can remember that, why can't I remember the rest of it? Why can't I remember this place? Or you?" His eyes shifted to the swell below her heart. "Or this baby?"

Erin bit her lip, debating. "I can answer the last part. It's because you didn't know about the baby. I . . . was saving that . . . as a surprise."

She couldn't bring herself to tell him about the argument. That she had been all set to tell him about the baby, but had backed away when they had gotten into a heated discussion about the morality of bringing a child into a world filled with discord and disease. Maybe if—*when*—he regained his memory, that part would still remain unavailable to him.

It would be all right, she thought, if he didn't remember that part of it.

He was looking at her, waiting. Erin cleared her throat. "I never got the opportunity to tell you."

This had to be difficult for her, Brady thought. The dated photographs in her album indicated that they had been together for some time.

But he had no answers, only questions. "Did I live here with you?"

She smiled ruefully. "We talked about your moving in. To all intents and purposes, you practically had." His clothes hung in her closet; his robe was still beside hers on one of the twin hooks on the bathroom door. But he had never asked her to marry him. She shrugged. If she was going to bring him back, it would be with the truth. "You found it difficult to commit sometimes."

If he didn't live here, then where? He frowned, rising. "Where did I live?"

"In an apartment in Newport Beach." But not anymore. "That is, you did." Brady looked puzzled. "After you didn't return, the landlord eventually had to rent out your apartment."

"My things?" He assumed that he must have accumulated some possessions, although nothing stood out in his mind.

"I have them," she assured him quickly. "I put some things in storage for you. The rest are here." She nodded toward the back. "In the spare bedroom." Her hand braced on the table, Erin rose. "Would you like to look through them?"

"Yes," he said slowly. "Yes, I would." Brady wanted to see anything and everything that would help ease him out of this cloudy prison he couldn't seem to break out of on his own.

"Okay, it's this way." Erin reached for his hand automatically, then dropped it when he looked at her curiously. "Sorry, habit."

He surprised her by reaching for her hand. She raised her eyes to his quizzically. "Then do it. Do everything that you did with me before I...went away. I want my life back—" Brady stopped abruptly, searching for her name. In his agitation, it had slipped away from him.

He couldn't remember her name, she realized. "Erin," she supplied patiently. "Erin Collins."

"I want my life back, Erin," he told her with feeling. "And I can't get it back alone."

This was new, she thought. She couldn't remember a time when Brady had asked her for help. Her fingers tightened around his.

"I'll do anything I can," she promised. "You know that."

"No," Brady contradicted her as she led him to the other bedroom. "I don't know that."

Erin laughed. That was more like it, she thought. "See? You're beginning to act like your old self already."

She'd lost him. He had a vague suspicion that she did that a lot. "How so?"

She slipped her hand from his and touched his cheek lightly. Lovingly. "Brady Lockwood is a very, very logical person. Sometimes maddeningly so." Alone in bed at night, she'd gone over every single moment they had shared. All his faults had become virtues. She'd sworn to herself that if he ever returned, she would be more patient. "Everything has a beginning and an ending for you," she said softly. "A reason for being."

A shadow of a memory whispered along his mind when she touched him like that. But it had no form, no substance. He let it pass, knowing the harder he tried, the less he succeeded.

"But you're not like that?" he guessed by her intonation.

"No, I'm not like that," she agreed. "I tend to be mercurial. Impulsive." A smile slid along her lips. "It drove you crazy sometimes."

It didn't make sense to him. "Then why did we stay together?"

Erin stopped before the bedroom door and turned toward him. That was so like him. To question the logic. There wasn't any. What there had been, and would be again, were feelings.

"Because you loved me, Brady. And I loved you." She looked up into his eyes.

Brady felt so helpless. "I wish I could say—"

She placed a finger to his lips, stopping him. She didn't want to hear him tell her that he didn't feel anything. Though she understood his confusion, the words would hurt too much.

"You will," she vowed with such passion that it took him by surprise. "You will."

Turning, Erin opened the door for him. But he remained where he was. "You're a lot more certain of that than I am."

Erin lifted a shoulder carelessly and let it drop. "Fools rush in—" she began, quoting something he liked to recite to her.

"—where angels fear to tread," Brady said automatically. Then he stopped, surprised at his own response.

Erin grabbed his hand and squeezed. "See?" she cried. "You're in there, Brady. You're in this large, sealed room, looking for a way out." Her eyes caressed him lovingly, eagerly. "And I know you. You'll find a crack that you'll force open. That's where the stubbornness comes in."

Brady looked at the set of her chin. "Are you stubborn?"

She led the way into the room. "You always told me I was. Too stubborn." She echoed words he had said to her more than once, sometimes lovingly, sometimes not.

Good. He had a feeling she was going to need that stubbornness. And so was he. "Then don't give up on me, Erin."

Her eyebrows rose in surprise. Give up? After she had found him? No way.

Impulsively, she did what she had been wanting to do since she'd first seen him today. She threaded her arms around his neck. "I have no intention of giving up on you. Ever."

He realized that he was moving on instinct. Instinct that came from some hidden recess within him. Instinct that had a better memory than he did. Brady's arms went around Erin as he lowered his mouth to hers.

It was a kiss comprising gratitude and curiosity. Need and exploration. He kissed her because it seemed to be the thing to do, and because he wanted to know what it felt like.

Brady kissed her because he wanted to jar his memory. And because he simply wanted to.

Though he still didn't know her, there was no denying that there was something about her that pulled him toward her, an attraction that was almost magnetic in nature. He didn't know if it was the sad look in her eyes or the way her mouth quirked. Or the fact that he desperately wanted to reclaim what had once been his and know it as his own again.

Erin could have cried. But she didn't. Instead, she lost herself in the delicious sensations that immediately leaped in her veins. The chemistry that had burned brightly between them was still there, despite the fact that the kiss began almost politely. It ignited, catching fire like a candle being lit by a flame thrower.

Why had he no memory of this woman? Her kiss rocked Brady to his very toes, spreading like liquid fire through his body.

The kiss quickly deepened, pulling them both in.

It was there, she thought, rising to her toes. The fire, the emotions, everything. His mind might be sleeping, but his soul was still there, and it belonged to her.

4

It seemed as if an eternity had passed before Brady finally stepped back. Stunned by the impact he felt, he looked down at Erin. The kiss had been an instinctive, unpremeditated action, like breathing. He had given it no thought. It had just happened.

When he kissed her, he had expected it to be pleasant, interesting. Nice. What he hadn't expected was to be knocked for a loop. Yet that was exactly what had happened.

"Wow." He took a deep breath and then exhaled, shaking his head as if to clear it. "You'd think a man would remember something like that."

Her hands on his forearms, Erin all but rocked on the balls of her feet. Excitement surged through her. He kissed like Brady. Exactly like Brady. Some part of him was operating on automatic pilot. It was only a matter of time before he healed and remembered everything.

"Do you?" she asked eagerly, searching his face for a sign. "Just a little?"

Brady wanted to say yes just to set her mind at ease, but he couldn't bring himself to lie to her. He had a feeling that he wouldn't have. Besides, it wouldn't be fair. She would see through it soon enough if he lied.

"No." He smiled into her face. With long, gentle fingers, he swept back the hair that had fallen into her eyes. As he cupped her cheek, the moment hummed of intimacy. "But I think I would like to work on re- calling that particular memory."

Her breath caught for a moment. The man before her was Brady and yet, he wasn't, she thought. Brady had never been this forward the first time around. Not when they were first hammering out a relationship. Maybe this "new" Brady would evolve until he merged the best qualities of the man he had been with the one who had just kissed her.

The one who didn't know her, but wanted to.

Heartened, hopeful, Erin returned his smile. His words created an odd thrill. In a way, she was falling in love with him all over again. "Do you want to look through your things now?"

He nodded, but as she began to walk into the room, Brady didn't follow.

Erin turned toward him, puzzled. Was he remem- bering something, after all? She laid her hand on his arm. "What is it?"

He looked past her head into the room. A room he'd never seen before. "What if I don't remember?" He looked into her eyes. "What if I look through everything and still don't remember?"

Erin wished she could wipe his fear away for him. She could only guess how horrible it had to be for him, not knowing. It wasn't exactly a picnic for her, either.

"You will. If not today, then tomorrow, or the day after. You'll be walking down the street, and it'll suddenly play back in your head like a delayed videotape."

Brady's eyes held hers, mesmerized. He was surprised by the intensity he saw there.

She'd never believed anything so vehemently in her life. "I promise, you will."

A smile played on Brady's lips despite the gravity of his situation. "And you can make a guarantee like that to me."

Erin didn't hesitate for an instant. She raised her chin. "I can."

Amusement warred with bewilderment at the illogic of her statement. "How?"

There were no words to explain the feeling she had in the center of her soul. But as surely as the sun rose in the morning, Erin believed that Brady's memory would return. They'd had something too precious for him not to remember eventually. She refused to believe that something that good could be lost forever.

Erin spread her hands innocently. "I just can, that's all."

He laughed shortly as he shook his head. "You're right. You're not very logical."

It wasn't anything that she hadn't heard from his lips a dozen times before. Her eyes shone. "I don't have to be. I'm pregnant."

He wondered why her attitude didn't irritate him. He assumed it should have. Instead, he found it oddly endearing. "Something tells me that you weren't logical even before you were pregnant."

Was he having a breakthrough, or just teasing her? "Then you remember?"

Did he? No, this was something he was surmising, based on the behavior he was witnessing, Brady decided. "Not exactly."

But that was what she wanted. Exactly. She wanted him to remember everything exactly the way it had happened. It was asking a lot, she realized. Even at his best, Brady tended to be forgetful. She'd once said that he only remembered Christmas because it was preceded by months of advertising.

Erin threaded her hand through his and led Brady into the room. "C'mon, let me take you down memory lane. Hopefully," she added under her breath.

But he heard. Her sentiment echoed his own.

Brady spent the next two hours in the room with her, sifting through all the things she told him were his. It did no good. His own possessions did no more to activate his memory than her house had.

A few items, when he touched or examined them, had stirred something in his mind in a vague sort of way. Like the worn sweatshirt she told him he'd always favored wearing around the house on Sundays. But the feeling was more like the numb buzzing across the sole of a foot that had fallen asleep. There hadn't been anything more concrete to it than that.

Erin fingered the mystery book Brady had been reading when he disappeared. He'd forgotten to pack it for his trip. She had to concentrate to suppress her disappointment as she looked at him. His was almost palpable.

"It's too soon to expect you to remember." Erin dug her knuckles into the surface of the bed as she began to get up. These days, that was becoming harder and harder for her to do, especially when she was sitting on something soft.

Brady rose and automatically took her arm, helping her to her feet. The gesture was so reminiscent of others, she couldn't understand why it didn't trigger something inside of him.

But it didn't. She could see it in his eyes. "Thank you," she said softly.

Brady nodded. Reluctantly, he released her arm. He was about to say something, when the doorbell rang. "That's Gus."

A flutter of unease wound through her at the sound of the bell. She caught his arm as he began to leave the room.

"Would you like to stay here tonight?" she suggested again. Her own voice sounded a tad too eager to her ear, but there was no time to build up to this moment. She continued quickly. "In here, with your things?'' Erin gestured behind her. "Maybe everything might seem clearer to you in the morning.''

It made sense, but he couldn't stay. "I have to go to work,'' Brady reminded her. Until he could reclaim the world that had been lost to him, he wanted to remain connected to the one he had grown to know.

Erin wasn't going to take no for an answer. She really didn't want to see him walk away again, not with evening sweeping along the streets. Not when so much reminded her of the last time. "I can drive you.''

He shook his head, walking out of the room. "No, I don't want to impose, Erin.''

Erin stopped abruptly. When she caught his arm again, turning him around, he was surprised at the strength and urgency he felt in her grip. And more surprised by the fierceness in her expression.

"Don't you get it yet?'' After kissing her, after feeling what she was sure he had felt, what *she* had felt, she didn't understand how he could say that. "We're not just polite acquaintances. We were lovers,'' she cried. Taking his hand, she placed it on her abdomen. "This is your baby in here. You're not 'imposing.' Imposing is for a third cousin twice removed from Chicago who wants to spend three weeks in your spare bedroom, not someone you were going to build a future with.''

Her words seemed to vibrate through him. "Were we building a future together?''

"Yes.''

It was understood, if not spoken. At least, Erin had thought it was understood. They were going to build forever together. That was why she had been so upset to learn how he actually felt about bringing a child into the world. He liked children. She had naturally thought that he would have liked one of his own. One of *their* own. Especially since there was one in the offing.

The doorbell rang again. Brady looked toward the door and then toward Erin. Her hand was still on his arm. Maybe she was right. Maybe waking up in what should be familiar surroundings to him might make him remember something. And even if it didn't, it seemed to be important to her that he remain.

"All right," he agreed. "I'll stay."

"Good." She exhaled a sigh of relief. Her mind went into high gear again. Thoughts, ideas, began to take shape in her head at a prodigious rate. Her tongue, as always, was ahead of them. "And then, tomorrow afternoon after work," she said pointedly, "I'm going to take you to the lab. Maybe something there will jar your memory, even if your possessions and I can't."

That settled, Erin smiled brightly and went to open the door for Gus.

Brady had woken up early every morning and wondered if that was something he had done before he'd lost his memory. This morning, he opened his eyes and stared at the ceiling. Slowly, he focused on his surroundings. That same, strange buzzing sound that greeted him each morning was in his ears, that same feeling of helpless disorientation. It had been with him ever since he had come to in that alley, divested of his possessions and his life.

Brady dug his elbows into the mattress and propped himself up. This wasn't the room behind the kitchen. He wasn't at Aphrodite's.

Where was he?

Brady sat up, looking around. There was white molding along the walls, butted up against the ceiling.

Blue walls. Blue paint. An overturned can and paint spattered on his shoes. No, not shoes, sneakers. New sneakers. Laughter. He could hear it, feel it....

And then it was gone.

Damn it, why didn't these flashes remain for more than a fleeting second, long enough for him to make sense of them?

But they were almost always gone before he realized they were there.

He blew out a long breath, dragging a hand through his hair. Another morning in wonderland, he thought, resigning himself.

The buzzing in his head subsided. It transformed into another noise. Tapping, no knocking. Someone was knocking on his door.

Erin.

"Yes?"

Her first instinct had been to open the door. Prudence made her knock, instead. One small step at a time, she thought. It was so hard, when all she wanted to do was run.

"Brady? It's Erin. Are you up?"

Hers was the most incredibly chipper tone he'd ever heard. It was like listening to the sound of morning birds.

"No, I'm sleeping," he quipped, smiling to himself. He found himself looking forward to seeing her. To seeing her smile fill his room. "Yes, I'm up."

As soon as he said it, the door flew open. Erin came in, a long pink robe draped over her body, tied with a satin sash that looked vaguely familiar to him. The hem of the robe whispered along the rug as she came in. Her hair was slightly tousled, and she smelled of sleep, soap and exuberance.

"I was just checking," she admitted. Erin stood a few steps inside the room, content for the moment just to look at him. "I thought maybe I had dreamed this. That you were back," she explained.

"At least in body," he murmured. Brady swung his legs over the side of the bed. He almost stood up when he remembered that he wasn't wearing anything. He quickly pulled the covers back over himself.

Erin grinned at his sudden outburst of modesty. "I've seen it before." Her hand cupped over her belly for emphasis.

"Yes," Brady agreed, "but I don't remember showing it."

She laughed. Sleeping in the nude was something new. Brady tended toward pajama bottoms. Some changes, she mused, were apparently for the better. She smiled at him. He was waiting for her to leave before getting dressed. Erin moved toward the door.

"I'm going to make breakfast for us. French toast." That had been his favorite.

Brady waved his hand at the offer. "Just plain toast and coffee," he told her. "I don't eat much in the morning."

Erin turned to look at him just before she closed the door. "Yes, you do—did." *Don't push.* She sighed. "Plain toast it is."

"No," he called, stopping her. The only way he was going to remember anything, he thought, was if he did everything the way he had done it before. "Make it your way."

"It's yours, too, Brady," she reminded him as she walked out.

Maybe, he thought, staring at the closed door, but he didn't know it. He started to get up just as Erin reentered the room. He yanked the sheet strategically into place again.

"Do you do this often?" he asked in exasperation.

"No, but I might start." A grin playing on her lips, Erin addressed her words to the ceiling. "You can take a shower in my bathroom." She crossed her heart. "I promise I won't come in."

Famous last words, he thought.

When Brady entered the kitchen fifteen minutes later, his hair was still damp. It curled invitingly around his ears and neck. Erin longed to run her fingers through it the way she once had.

She was right, he thought. The smell of French toast aroused his dormant appetite. He noticed an odd expression on her face. "What's wrong?"

"Déjà vu," she answered. She turned back to the stove and flipped the slices in the skillet a final time. "At least for me. You've come padding in barefoot like that in the morning dozens of times. I was just thinking how good it was to see you doing that again."

She took out two plates and placed them on the counter. With a quick turn of the spatula, she divided their breakfast. "Find everything you needed in the bathroom?" she asked conversationally.

"Yes. Was that robe on the hook—"

"Yours," she confirmed.

He nodded to himself as he glanced at the clock on the wall. "It's almost seven. I have to be at the restaurant by eight. Demi serves brunch."

Erin couldn't help wondering, despite Gus's assurance, what else Demi might have served Brady these past months.

No, she admonished herself, that train of thought had no place here. The last thing she needed to be was jealous. Quick, helpful, resourceful—she had to be all those things, but not jealous.

"I can get ready as soon as we finish eating," she promised. Picking up a plate in each hand, she turned around.

He looked dubiously at her robe. She wasn't even dressed yet.

Erin found that she could still read his thoughts. That was very heartening. She placed a plate in front of him. "I'm very fast when I have to be. That used to always surprise you." She smiled. "I guess it still does."

Setting down her own plate, Erin sat down. She paused a moment just to absorb the sight of Brady eating.

He felt her eyes on him. His fork hovered over the plate. "I eat better without an audience."

"Sorry." But she couldn't help smiling. This felt wonderful, Erin thought gratefully. Everything else would fall into place as they went along.

She just knew it.

It had been one of the longest days he'd endured since he found himself walking along that dark, empty alley. Dark, empty, like the recesses of his mind. Each hour had literally crawled by on scrapped knees, even though it had been packed at the restaurant and he'd been working almost nonstop from nine until Erin had picked him up at four.

He'd been waiting for her to return ever since she pulled away from the curb that morning. The word *physicist* had been rolling across the planes of his mind like a marble searching for a niche to lodge in. Something told Brady that he was standing just on the brink.

He looked at her now as she drove him to Edmond Labs. Questions were multiplying in his mind. "Why did you keep my possessions?"

That was a strange question. She would have thought that the answer would be rather obvious to him. "Well, I couldn't very well let them be thrown out."

He was doing his best to understand. "But you thought I walked out on you. On everyone," he amended, trying to make sense of what she was saying. Given that, surely another woman would have thrown everything away. "Weren't you angry?"

She smiled, remembering for both of them. "At first," she admitted. "But then I started thinking that it wasn't like you to just leave, no matter how angry you might have been—"

He still hadn't gotten all the details of that last day. "Why was I angry?"

She'd tripped herself up this time, Erin thought. Her mind scrambled for damage control as she tried to read the street signs. She'd only traveled this route a few times before.

"You know that discussion I mentioned we had the last day..."

"Yes?"

"Well, actually, it was more like an argument," she said cautiously.

"About what?" Brady prodded when Erin didn't continue.

"Nothing specific," she lied, hoping that he would forgive her later if he eventually remembered the content of the argument. She shrugged carelessly. "Just one of those things that blows up out of nothing." Maybe once the baby was born, he would look at it that way.

Brady tried to visualize arguing with her and couldn't. "Did that happen a lot with us?"

She was relieved that she could be truthful again. "No, as a matter of fact, that was the only time." She gave him the details that she had gone over a hundred times in her mind in the last five months. "You left to cool off. You were going to St. Louis on a business trip the next day, so when you didn't come back that night, I thought you were still angry. Then *I* got really angry because you hadn't said goodbye to me."

Pride had been behind that, she thought ruefully. Stupid pride. If she hadn't let it get in the way, she could have started looking for him immediately.

"You were only supposed to be gone for two weeks. After three passed, I finally went to your apartment. Your car was still gone, and I thought that maybe you really had decided to stay in St. Louis." She licked her lower lip. "Before you left, you said something about staying in St. Louis permanently. I thought it was just anger talking, but when you didn't return, I flew up there to look for you."

She remembered it vividly. The odd look on the desk clerk's face when she'd asked if Brady had checked out the week before. The man had indignantly recalled that Brady hadn't had the decency to cancel the reservation he never made use of. She remembered, too, the awful feeling in the pit of her stomach as she'd sat in the back of the taxi on her way to the police station.

"You never checked into your hotel. I filed a missing person's report on you that afternoon with the St. Louis police."

"St. Louis?" he repeated. "Why didn't you file it in Bedford?" That seemed only logical to him.

"Because I didn't think you were here. The airlines told me, after a great deal of pleading on my part," she explained, "that you had used your ticket. You had flown to St. Louis."

Looking back, she realized that it must have been the mugger who had flown in Brady's place, or maybe it was someone the mugger had either sold or given the tickets to.

He didn't remember flying to St. Louis. "Gus found me here." He gave her a date that corresponded to the day after he had left her apartment.

She stopped at the light and leaned out the window to read the street sign.

"All the time I was looking for you in St. Louis, you were here." Erin shook her head. There was no sense in agonizing over it now. "But that's all behind us."

That was just the problem, Brady thought. He had no idea what was behind him. "And what's in front?"

She wanted to say "us," but that part would eventually be up to him. She wanted Brady to love her, to remember loving her and to accept both her and the baby. But she couldn't *make* him. And even if she could, she wouldn't. It wouldn't mean anything. He had to come to her on his own.

She glanced at him, a bright smile she didn't quite feel on her face. "A reeducation, starting with the lab where you worked. I called Mr. Waverly this morning and explained everything to him."

Erin had called the head of Brady's former department as soon as she had arrived at the flower shop this morning.

The name meant nothing to him, even as he repeated it. "Waverly?"

"He was your boss." She could almost hear Brady trying to remember. She'd met Jacob Waverly only once, at a Christmas party he had given. She'd had to coerce Brady into going. He liked small gatherings, not large parties. She was at home anywhere.

Erin tried to summon the man's image in her mind. "Tall, skinny man. Looks like the model for Icabod Crane." Another reference he probably didn't know. She sighed. "Never mind."

But Brady knew that anything, no matter how insignificant, might somehow be the catalyst to opening the door to his past. "What?"

"Icabod Crane," she repeated. "You probably don't know what I'm talking about."

It was so odd what he could remember and what he couldn't. The morning after his mugging, he'd had to look at a newspaper to know what state he was in, but he knew without doubt what Erin was referring to.

"Legend of Sleepy Hollow, right?"

She beamed. "Right." Erin came to another light and looked at him curiously. "You know that?"

She was no more mystified than he was. He watched the road intently as she began to drive again. "Erin, there are so many pieces floating around in my head. I know some things without knowing how. Other things..." He shrugged. "There's no rhyme or reason to it." He certainly couldn't find one.

Brady glanced to his left. She was going to miss the turn. "Make a left." He pointed. "There."

He was pointing to a turn in the middle of the road. The next light was at the end of the block. She remembered that she had to make a left at the signal. "The entrance is up ahead."

He knew that, he thought. He *knew* that. "Yes, but there's a side one, as well. Duffy's on du...ty."

Brady stretched out the word as the impact of what he was saying hit him like a starburst right between the eyes. Shock mingled with relief and extreme pleasure.

"I remember, Erin," he said excitedly. "I remember Duffy." Then, as if to prove it to her—and maybe himself—he began describing the man. "Full head of white hair, big grin. Always had a story."

Erin turned where he told her to. Sure enough, there was a guard's gate in the distance. Her heart hammering, she pulled over to the side of the compound. Her fingers were trembling as she yanked up the emergency brake. The car idled in Park.

He wanted to see Duffy with his own eyes, to see someone he had suddenly remembered knowing. "What are you doing?" he demanded.

Erin didn't answer. Instead, she leaned over the bucket seat and hugged him as hard as she could. "I don't care if you remembered a funny white-haired old man and not me. You remembered something. You remembered, and that's all that matters."

Blinking back tears, she kissed him. The lump in her throat was huge and it took effort to squeeze the words out. "You remembered."

Overwhelmed by the moment and by her display of affection, Brady could say nothing. He was vaguely aware that another woman would have been hurt that he couldn't remember *her* but did remember a wizened old guard. Brady looked at her thoughtfully for a long moment. The lady was really something else.

Sniffing, Erin drew back into her seat. She shifted the car into drive and released the brake.

"Okay, now let's see what else we can get you to remember."

"Erin," he said softly, "I'm sorry I can't remember . . . us."

She pretended to shrug it off. "That's all right. You'll make it up to me when you finally do." She glanced at him. "You're that type."

He settled back in his seat again. "I'll take your word for it."

Erin drove toward the entrance and the guard's small booth. Just as Brady had said, a white-haired man emerged from his station, a clipboard in his hands.

Duffy, she thought, bless him.

5

"**M**r. Lockwood!" The pleasure in Duffy's gravelly voice was unmistakable. The old security guard leaned over, peering in through the open window on Erin's side. He extended a gnarled hand to Brady and shook it with feeling. "Where have you been? I thought for sure you'd left us."

Brady exchanged looks with Erin. "In a way, I guess I did."

Duffy's keen sky-blue eyes shifted to Erin. The cloud of confusion disappeared from his face immediately. "Ah, well, now, I can see why that would be. Is this the missus then?"

Erin didn't wait for Brady to refute the guard's assumption. "Mr. Waverly is expecting us," she told Duffy. "He said he'd put us on the list."

With a flourish, Duffy flipped through the papers on his clipboard. "Sure, there you are." The old man tapped a blunt index finger at the line with their names on it. "Right here on line twenty-two. Brady Lockwood and Erin Collins," he read. His eyes shifted to Erin. "You'd be *Ms*. Collins then?" She nodded.

He beamed at Brady as he handed two visitor badges to them before retreating. "Good to see you again, Mr. Lockwood."

Brady nodded. "You don't know how good it is to see *you*." How good it was to see *someone* who was vaguely familiar.

Duffy leaned into the booth and pressed a button on the control panel. The gate slowly retracted, allowing them entrance onto the compound.

"Go on in." He waved them forward. The guard chuckled to himself as he passed a hand over his pointed chin. "I don't have to tell you where to go."

Erin bit her lower lip. She spoke quickly to spare Brady the frustration of admitting to yet someone else that he had lost his memory. "I'm afraid that this time, you do."

Duffy's white eyebrows drew together like winter clouds preparing to drop snow on the ground. He scratched the front of his head, pondering the remark. The navy blue cap perched precariously on the back of his head threatened to fall off. He tugged it back into place.

"Okay. It's the third building on the left. The squat one with two floors," he added for good measure, pointing out the building.

"Room 230," Brady said suddenly. The number materialized in his mind's eye as Erin drove the car through the gate.

He was trying so hard, she thought, sympathy curling through her. Erin shook her head. "No, we're meeting Waverly in his office. Room 211."

She didn't understand. "I mean, where I used to work. My office. It's room 230." He could visualize it, though why that and nothing else, he didn't begin to comprehend. Brady closed his eyes for a second. The window. He remembered the window. His eyes opened, filled with surprise. "It overlooks an atrium."

Yes! Erin thought.

Emotion danced through her as she drove toward the building Duffy had pointed out. "I'm sure it's a wonderful atrium."

Jacob Waverly did look as if he had posed for Icabod Crane some thirty years ago. He presented a tall, gaunt appearance even when he was sitting down. His thin, patrician face was sunken-in, despite the amount of pasta he liked to consume during his frequent lunches at the Italian restaurant located a few blocks away.

Right now, a smile reposed on it, and his eyes were kindly behind his thick-lensed glasses as his secretary ushered in Erin and Brady.

Waverly quickly rose from behind his steel desk and clasped Brady's hand heartily in his. With a nod of his head, he dismissed his secretary. "I can't tell you how happy I am to see you, Lockwood."

There was no doubting the genuineness of his words. He'd assured Erin when she called to tell him about Brady's condition that Brady was respected and liked by everyone. He was eager to do anything he could to help.

"We all thought you were—well, never mind what we all thought." He waved the matter away. "It was wrong."

He'd believed, as had others, that Brady had been killed in St. Louis, to become one of those unsolved crimes that haunted the annals of crime files. Waverly had been extremely pleased to receive Erin's telephone call this morning.

"Sit, sit." Waverly gestured to the chair directly behind Brady. "And you, too, of course, Ms. Collins." He took in her very obvious condition with surprise. "Due any day now, I imagine."

She hadn't thought she looked that large. "Not for another month."

Waverly nodded, barely hearing her, as his attention shifted to Brady.

"Ms. Collins told me about...the 'problem.'" His voice had dropped a decibel when he uttered the euphemism. "I want you to know that I'm prepared to help in any way necessary." Waverly placed a fatherly hand on Brady's shoulder. "It just hasn't been the same without you here. No one seems to know as much as I thought they did." He chuckled softly.

Erin looked at Brady, jumping ahead to what she hoped was a logical conclusion based on what Waverly intimated. "His work was always very important to Brady. I thought, perhaps, if Brady could come back here to work, to observe," she amended, "it might help him remember. He already remembered Duffy," she added quickly, hoping that would support her suggestion.

Waverly laughed. "I shouldn't wonder. Duffy's a hard man to forget. Talks up a storm, given half a chance. I imagine everyone on the compound will know you're back by this time tomorrow."

The man paused, seriously considering Erin's suggestion. Waverly leaned a hip against the desk and looked at Brady thoughtfully. "Are you back, Lockwood? Are you ready to come back?"

Brady looked around the office slowly, taking in every last detail and searching for a match within his mind. It looked distantly familiar, as if he'd seen this all in a dream once, but where and when continued to remain unclear.

His eyes came to rest on Waverly. The man was watching him, waiting patiently. "I'd like to," Brady answered.

That seemed to be all Waverly needed to hear. He straightened. "Here, why don't we go to your former office and then to the lab so you can look around?" He was already leading the way to the door, then paused as he looked back at Erin. "You can remain here if you'd prefer."

But Erin was already on her feet. "No, I prefer to remain with him," she assured Waverly as she took Brady's arm.

She didn't intend to miss one step of this uncharted journey Brady had to undertake. If work, not her, was the trigger that set him off, fine, she could deal with that. All she wanted was for Brady to be himself again.

It was coming back to him, at least a small shred of a memory. When he walked into his office, Brady knew exactly where things were supposed to be. But when he opened a drawer, the folders inside were unfamiliar to him. It was just like receiving a blow to the pit of his stomach. The disappointment was almost devastating. He'd been so sure.

Brady shoved his hands into his pockets, masking his frustration. "I guess I don't remember, after all."

"No, no," Waverly assured him quickly. "Pierpont moved into your office when you didn't return. He's boxed some of your things. We can have maintenance bring them up again."

Brady looked at Erin. "Then I do remember."

She smiled at him as she threaded her hand through his. This had been a great idea, she congratulated herself. "Yes, you do."

It hadn't taken long for word to spread throughout the building. The floor was fairly honeycombed with small, partitioned cubblyholes that served as offices for the backbone of Edmond Labs, and it seemed everyone had known Brady. Within minutes, the area was flooded with people who had interacted with him on a daily basis. Greetings and exclamations of surprise came from all directions.

Brady didn't recognize any of them, and the strain was telling.

Erin looked at Waverly for help, and the man read the imploring look in her eyes.

"Why don't we go down to the main lab?" Waverly suggested. Brady gratefully allowed himself to be ushered away.

Waverly silently observed Brady as he moved through the laboratory with a familiarity that was so ingrained, it seemed second nature to him. Apparently you could take the man out of the physicist, but you couldn't take the physicist out of the man, Waverly thought.

"Why don't we do what Ms. Collins suggested?" he proposed to Brady. "Why don't you come back here, say, on a part-time basis, perhaps start working with an assistant on one of your old projects and see where that takes you." Waverly smiled at his own suggestion. "Something that wasn't due yesterday."

Brady nodded. "I'd really like that," he agreed.

"Then consider it done." To seal the bargain, Waverly shook Brady's hand.

The key was here, in this lab. Brady knew he could find himself here.

And then, perhaps, he thought as he looked at Erin, he could find the man that she had loved.

Erin was bursting with questions. She couldn't wait until they were alone again. She held out long enough for them to get to her car.

"How does it feel?" she asked as he buckled up. "Is some of it really coming back to you?" She started the car, waiting.

He couldn't begin to describe the way he felt, but it had to be akin to seeing a light at the end of a long, dark tunnel.

"Yes, it's all still sort of vague, but I felt as if I belonged there." He had scanned a report that Waverly had told him he'd written and while he didn't remember doing it, he could understand it. Brady laughed softly. "I guess the physics goes down deep."

She'd always said that. "Right to the bone," Erin responded, forcing a cheerful note into her voice.

She wasn't going to let it bother her, Erin thought with determination. She'd always known that she came second after his work. This just verified it. And if the pill had a bitter taste, she could still swallow it.

"Do I have a car?"

Brady's sudden question caught Erin off guard. She hadn't given his car any thought in months.

"I don't know," she said honestly. "I mean, you did, but it wasn't at your apartment complex. My guess is that whoever mugged you stole it, along with your airplane ticket. If it was abandoned, it's probably been stripped and recycled by now." Erin was thinking aloud. "We could ask Gus to check if the police found any abandoned vehicles." She glanced at him before driving away from the compound. "Why do you ask?"

This small crack he'd discovered in the wall that surrounded his memory excited Brady. He wanted to explore it further, push it for all it was worth to see where it would take him.

"Because I want to take Waverly up on his offer as soon as possible." Another thought occurred to him. "To begin with, I guess I should find out if I can still drive."

She backed up and tried to approach the problem logically. The irony of that amused her.

"We can go to the DMV and get you another copy of your driver's license." Doing a quick calculation in her head, she decided she could probably take him there tomorrow afternoon. "Until you get it, I can drive you." Erin slanted a look at him, hesitating before she continued, "Especially if you move in."

She'd been thinking about that all day. Waking up and finding him there this morning had been like an answer to a prayer.

Brady made no response, so she hurried on, "It only makes sense. You'll need a place to stay if you're not working at the restaurant," she reminded him. "And the more you surround yourself with what was once familiar to you, the greater the chance of your coming across something that will make you remember more than a white-haired old man and an atrium."

He knew that Demi would let him stay in the room he now occupied for as long as he needed. Both she and Gus were extraordinary people. But Erin had a point. He needed to have the familiar around him at all times. He was anxious to have this mystery existence he was living over with as soon as possible. Moving in with Erin only made sense.

Besides, there was no getting around the fact that he was attracted to her. Really attracted. He didn't know that much about himself, but he did know that there was something about Erin he found enormously appealing. Being with her felt right, just the way being in the lab had been.

"All right," he agreed. "Seeing as how you have most of my things, anyway, that only makes sense."

Score one for the short redhead. "Absolutely," she answered with a grin. "Logical to the very end."

She was about to pass the last entrance to Westminister Mall before the freeway on-ramp when she suddenly decided to turn in.

The west-end parking lot of the large indoor mall was almost empty. In between holidays and sales, shopping should be light at this time of the evening, she decided. It was the perfect place.

Brady looked around. This didn't look familiar to him, either. Why was she stopping here?

"What are you doing?" If he had learned nothing else in the last day and a half, he had learned that Erin was completely unpredictable.

"You said you wanted to know if you remembered how to drive." She pulled up the emergency hand brake and shifted the car into park, but left it running. "No time like the present to find out." As he watched, stunned, Erin struggled out of the car. She looked at him expectantly. He was certainly slow on the uptake. "Switch places with me."

Brady got out slowly, uncertain about what she proposed. "What?"

"I said, switch places with me. You can find out if you remember what to do." Erin looked around the nearly deserted lot. "There aren't any parked cars to run into, and there's plenty of room to make a good-size turn if you want to practice."

She had a point. Brady rounded the hood and slid in behind the steering wheel. He was surprised when she began getting in on the passenger side. He'd assumed that when she said switch places, she meant for him to be in the driver's seat instead of her, but not that she would be in his seat. He would risk himself, but not her.

"Maybe you should just stay out and observe." He waited for her to get out.

She wasn't about to go anywhere. Erin had a feeling that, as he had at the laboratory, Brady would revert to automatic pilot once he started driving. She wasn't the least bit concerned. She supposed that he probably wouldn't think that was logical, but then, if she'd learned nothing else from him in all this time, it was that men and women approached situations differently. Especially if that woman was in love.

"Someone's got to watch to see if you do it right," she countered.

He knew she wasn't about to get out. Brady shook his head, surrendering. He had a feeling he was no match for her when she got going. "You have an answer for everything, don't you?"

Erin grinned. "Pretty much." He was learning. Or it was coming back to him. Either way, things were looking up.

Brady sat in the driver's seat, slowly running his hands down the steering wheel and then back up again. He tried to remember if there was another time when he'd sat just like this.

He couldn't recall, but it didn't feel unfamiliar to him. He supposed that was something.

Closing his eyes, he concentrated for a moment.

Brady eased the hand brake down and then shifted into drive. His foot moved from the brake pedal to the accelerator. The car began to move very slowly toward the end of the lot.

"See, what did I tell you?" Erin cried, beaming. She'd never doubted him for a moment. "It's like riding a bicycle."

He glanced at her. "I don't remember being able to do that, either."

She laughed. "There's a reason for that. You don't know how to ride a bicycle. It's just an expression."

"Oh."

Right after they found his memory, they were going to have to find his sense of humor. She watched him handle the car. "You're doing very well."

He thought she was patronizing him, but one look at her face told him that she was serious. He glanced at the speedometer. "At eleven miles an hour, I don't think I can do much damage."

Erin thought of the time her bumper had been creased by the car behind her just as the light had turned green. Impact had been at less than five miles an hour. "Oh, you'd be surprised."

"At this point—" Brady executed a U-turn with a minimum of effort and smiled to himself in satisfaction "—everything is a surprise to me."

Erin leaned over to get a better look at the speedometer. Fifteen miles an hour. He was still the same cautious man she had always loved.

"Why don't you try for twenty?" she urged.

"You're on." He went down one long row and then up another, following the arrows.

Erin nodded, pleased. "Well, I'm satisfied." She didn't feel like struggling out of the passenger seat to get behind the steering wheel again. "Would you like to drive home, Brady?"

It was one thing to drive around the lot, another to actually go out on the road. He thought of the legal ramifications. "But I don't have my license with me. What if we're stopped by a policeman?"

They were only seven miles from home. "Odds are against that, unless you suddenly decide to challenge someone to a drag race." Erin smiled to herself.

He liked her smile, he thought, even though he usually didn't know what brought it out. Like now. "What are you smiling about now?"

He was acting according to type, even though he wasn't aware of it. "The old Brady wouldn't have taken a chance either. He would have played it very safe." She waited for him to stop the car.

Brady drove down another lane, thinking. He wasn't certain if he liked the way she said that, or the implications that it held. He didn't care for the idea that he was completely predictable, especially when he didn't know what he was going to do himself.

He found himself wanting to be just a little reckless. Maybe it was because he chafed against the confines of the fog that held him prisoner. Maybe that was what made him want to break free.

Brady made up his mind.

"All right, I'll drive. But you're going to have to give me directions."

She was surprised. And pleased. "Every step of the way," she promised.

Brady had a feeling that she was talking about more than just the car ride. Somehow, she made him feel hopeful, an emotion that he didn't think he entertained very often.

There was something about her bubbly enthusiasm that made the road he was taking seem a little easier, a little less lonely.

"Ready for your solo flight, Mr. Lindbergh?" she teased. "The exit is just up ahead."

"It's my memory that's missing, not my eyesight," he told her. "And Lindbergh took his solo flight alone, hence the term 'solo.'"

"Testy." But she wasn't put off. He was trying hard not to smile, she noted.

Very cautiously, Brady eased his car onto the main road. Traffic was light, he observed gratefully. "When do you want me to move in?"

Yesterday.

She tried, unsuccessfully, to look subdued. "We could stop at the restaurant and tell Demi now," she suggested nonchalantly. "You know, pick up your things. Settle up." After all, this was the middle of the week, and he probably got paid on Friday.

Maybe she was going too fast, she thought when he didn't answer. "Unless you'd rather wait until tomorrow to do it."

Brady stopped the car at the light. The freeway entrance was just up ahead. He tried to remember the route she had taken here. North. He needed the entrance heading north, he thought. That minor hurtle conquered, he looked at her.

It bothered Brady a great deal that he couldn't tap into that area of his brain where memories of Erin were lodged. He knew that there had to be a great many, and he needed to get to them in order to feel whole.

The sooner the better. Maybe something that she would say or do tonight would make the difference and bring him back.

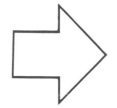

NO COST! NO OBLIGATION TO BUY! NO PURCHASE NECESSARY!

PLAY "LUCKY 7" AND GET FIVE FREE GIFTS!

HOW TO PLAY:

1. With a coin, carefully scratch off the silver box at the right. Then check the claim chart to see what we have for you—FREE BOOKS and a gift—ALL YOURS! ALL FREE!

2. Send back this card and you'll receive brand-new Silhouette Yours Truly™ novels. These books have a cover price of $3.50 each, but they are yours to keep absolutely free.

3. There's no catch. You're under no obligation to buy anything. We charge nothing—ZERO—for your first shipment. And you don't have to make any minimum number of purchases—not even one!

4. The fact is thousands of readers enjoy receiving books by mail from the Silhouette Reader Service™ months before they're available in stores. They like the convenience of home delivery and they love our discount prices!

5. We hope that after receiving your free books you'll want to remain a subscriber. But the choice is yours—to continue or cancel, anytime at all! So why not take us up on our invitation, with no risk of any kind. You'll be glad you did!

NOT ACTUAL SIZE

This beautiful porcelain box is topped with a lovely bouquet of porcelain flowers, perfect for holding rings, pins or other precious trinkets — and is yours absolutely free when you accept our no risk offer!

PLAY "LUCKY 7"

**Just scratch off the silver box with a coin.
Then check below to see the gifts you get.**

YES! I have scratched off the silver box. Please send me all the gifts for which I qualify. I understand I am under no obligation to purchase any books, as explained on the back and on the opposite page.

201 CIS AWPS
(U-SIL-YRT-02/96)

NAME

ADDRESS   APT.

CITY   STATE   ZIP

7	7	7	**WORTH FOUR FREE BOOKS PLUS A FREE PORCELAIN TRINKET BOX**
🍒	🍒	🍒	**WORTH THREE FREE BOOKS**
●	●	●	**WORTH TWO FREE BOOKS**
🔔	🔔	🍒	**WORTH ONE FREE BOOK**

Offer limited to one per household and not valid to current Silhouette Yours Truly™ subscribers. All orders subject to approval.

© 1990 HARLEQUIN ENTERPRISES LIMITED   **PRINTED IN U.S.A.**

THE SILHOUETTE READER SERVICE™: HERE'S HOW IT WORKS

Accepting free books places you under no obligation to buy anything. You may keep the books and gift and return the shipping statement marked "cancel". If you do not cancel, about a month later we'll send you 4 additional novels, and bill you just $2.69 each plus 25¢ delivery and applicable sales tax, if any.* That's the complete price, and—compared to cover prices of $3.50 each—quite a bargain! You may cancel at any time, but if you choose to continue, every other month we'll send you 4 more books, which you may either purchase at the discount price...or return at our expense and cancel your subscription.

*Terms and prices subject to change without notice. Sales tax applicable in N.Y.

BUSINESS REPLY MAIL
FIRST CLASS MAIL   PERMIT NO. 717   BUFFALO, NY

POSTAGE WILL BE PAID BY ADDRESSEE

SILHOUETTE READER SERVICE
3010 WALDEN AVE
PO BOX 1867
BUFFALO NY 14240-9952

NO POSTAGE
NECESSARY
IF MAILED
IN THE
UNITED STATES

If offer card is missing, write to: Silhouette Reader Service, 3010 Walden Ave., P.O. Box 1867, Buffalo, NY 14269-1867

"No," he told her as the light turned green, "I'd rather we did it tonight."

Content, Erin settled back in the seat. "You get on right there, just past the fast-food place," she directed calmly.

"I know. I watched the road when you drove here." Actually, he had watched *her* while they drove here. But the peripherals had managed to sink in.

"You're making progress." Erin began to hum to herself.

His head nearly snapped around as he looked at her sharply. "What's that?"

She looked at the road, alert. Had he spotted something? "What's what?"

"What you're humming."

Her heart settled into a normal pattern again. She paused, thinking. "I don't know." Erin hummed the refrain again. It was just one of those snatches of a tune that sometimes ran through her head. "Why, do you remember it?" she asked excitedly.

He thought he did, but then the feeling faded. He was trying too hard, it was just that he felt as if he were standing at a huge door that was barring him from the rest of his life. If he could only find a way to open it, if he could only find the right key, everything would be all right.

But he hadn't even the vaguest idea where the keyhole was.

"No," he murmured.

She noted the speedometer. "Um, about being stopped by the police—"

His eyes darted quickly to the rearview mirror. But there was no car with dancing red-and-blue lights following him. "What about it?"

"They stop you if you're going too slow, as well."

Murmuring something unintelligible under his breath, Brady pressed down harder on the accelerator.

6

→ ←

Brady eyed the tuxedo that Erin had brought in and laid out on his bed dubiously. Like almost everything else, he had no recollection of it, but he couldn't quite see himself wearing it.

"Are you sure this is mine?" he called out when he heard her shower door slam closed.

A minute later, Erin peered into his room. Her hair wrapped in a towel fashioned like a turban, she was wearing a blue bathrobe like the one that was hanging in his closet. Life with her hadn't returned to him, but Brady discovered that he was enjoying the one he was sharing now.

Erin felt as if she'd been running since dawn. They had exactly one hour to get to Marlene's house in order to be on time for the wedding. Weddings, she reminded herself. As planned, both Bailey sisters were getting married today at eleven. The flowers Marlene and Nicole had selected from her shop had been delivered by seven this morning. She'd been there to personally arrange the orchids, roses and carnations in the living room and the huge reception area.

The place had been in a state of what appeared to be organized chaos, with a small, gnomelike woman Marlene had introduced to her as Sally at the center of it, barking out orders to caterers and decorators alike. Erin had been grateful to do her part and then quickly slip out.

The flowers might have arrived on time, but she was having serious doubts right now if *they* would. Not if Brady insisted on looking at the tuxedo she had purchased as if it were the enemy.

"It's yours." She smiled at him reassuringly. "I'm positive." When the time came, Erin hoped he would forgive her this one little white lie, but he did look elegant wearing a tuxedo. She patted her hands along the outline of the turban, dabbing the excess moisture out of her hair. Mentally, she crossed her fingers. "It was at the cleaners. Maybe they shrank it or something."

He hadn't even tried putting on the suit yet. He picked it up and hooked the hanger on the top drawer so that the tuxedo draped against the armoire. The change in perspective didn't help. He still didn't care for it.

"No, it looks like it fits, but I'm not talking about that." He raised his eyes to hers. "It just doesn't look like the sort of thing that I'd wear."

Erin lifted the hanger and held the jacket against him. "Oh, you've worn it. And with aplomb." That much she didn't have to fabricate. "You look very dashing in it." She grinned. "And very sexy."

He didn't know about that. Glancing toward the mirror, Brady suspected the tuxedo made him look like a mannequin. He arched an eyebrow as he looked at the expression on her face. "You wouldn't be taking advantage of the situation now, would you?"

Erin exuded wide-eyed innocence, splaying a hand on her chest. "Who, me?"

Brady laughed and shook his head. She made him laugh a lot this past week. She added light to the gray world he was attempting to dig his way out of. Erin made this question mark he was living more than bearable. She made it all worthwhile.

He couldn't resist hooking a finger along her belt loop and pulling her closer to him. He liked the look of surprise that came into her eyes. Obviously, the gesture wasn't something he would have normally done. In an odd sort of way, that pleased him. Brady lightly brushed his lips along hers. Even that slight touch caused a spark to ripple through both of them, electricity waiting to be unleashed. Brady savored it a moment, then released her.

"Yes, you."

Erin stared at him, stunned. This was an untapped side of Brady, one she'd never seen before. One she really liked. A side she prayed she wouldn't have to give up once things became clear to him again.

It had been a week. One precious, wonderful week since he had reappeared in her life. A week since she had begun living again. In a way, it was still a little like residing in limbo, looking into his beautiful green eyes and not seeing the Brady she knew there.

But even that had its compensations. He was displaying qualities she'd never known he had. Qualities *he* probably didn't know he had. Qualities that made her fall in love with him all over again.

The main thing, she reminded herself, was that he was here. And, memory or no memory, he was still the man she loved.

When she'd picked him up at Edmond Labs that first afternoon, Erin had hoped that he would have experienced an epiphany of some sort sometime during the day. But although he told her that he continued to surprise himself with what he did know in terms of the work required of him, apart from Duffy and his office number, he still couldn't remember that he had ever worked at Edmond Labs. He'd read pages that he'd written and could actually follow the analyses and the mathematics involved. Yet he couldn't remember writing it. Recollection still seemed aeons away.

By now, she had come to grips with the fact that lightning wasn't going to strike. Brady wasn't going to look at her one morning and have everything suddenly come rushing back to him. She consoled herself with the fact that they were exploring each other all over again. That was pretty special in itself. How many people were given an opportunity to fall in love all over again?

At least, she thought looking at him, she hoped he was falling in love with her. She knew she already was in love with this new man, the one who was a little kinder, a little more sensitive, a little more vulnerable than the Brady who had once existed in his space.

She held the tuxedo up to him again. "Now stop looking at this as if it were a cobra and put it on. We have to hurry," she urged. She looked at the digital clock on his nightstand. "We're due at the wedding in less than an hour."

Pushing the tuxedo into his hands, she hurriedly left the room.

He sighed and laid the suit out on his bed again. The woman was a mystery, he mused. There was no doubt in his mind that he'd probably felt the same way about her before he'd been robbed of his memory.

"Do you attend all your clients' weddings?" he called out as he removed the hanger from the jacket.

Erin stuck her head in again. At this rate, she would never be ready. "No. But they're special. I met Marlene and Nicole at my doctor's office. They both just had babies," she added as a coda.

That seemed a little backward to him. "And they're getting married today?"

She knew how that must have sounded, but she'd been privy to both women's stories. She couldn't be happier at the outcome.

"It's rather an involved story," she assured him. Erin expected that to be the end of it.

Brady took out the shirt she had hung in the middle of his closet. Too much starch, he thought as he slipped it on.

"Really?" He raised his voice in case she couldn't hear him. "Well, maybe you can tell it to me on the way to the wedding."

Fingers flying as she put on her makeup, Erin abruptly paused. Brady didn't like long stories unless they had scientific significance. He tended to tune her out when she went on about something, which, she supposed, was only fair inasmuch as when he began talking about work, she usually glazed over no matter how hard she tried to pay attention.

Erin smiled as she lay down her eye shadow wand. She liked this new quality of his much better.

"You're on," she called back. "Now hurry."

Removing her robe, she quickly slipped on her undergarments. It was a struggle all the way. What had fit a month ago was now skintight. Just a little while longer, she promised herself, and she could start working her way down to all the clothes that were waiting for her in her closet.

Erin slid on her dress, a two-layered knee-length green number that tactfully hid just how large she had become. By Dr. Pollack's calculations, delivery was still three weeks away. Valentine's Day. She rather liked that, she mused. For the rest of her life, she was going to have her own personal valentine.

But in the meantime, she felt like a balloon.

The long sleeves fit more snugly than she was happy about. They also hindered her agility, already limited by her size. She could only pull up the zipper so far despite her contortions. It insisted on hiding somewhere between the small of her back and her shoulder blades.

If she tried any harder to get it, she was going to dislocate her shoulder, Erin thought in annoyance. She gave up. With a sigh, she marched down the small hallway to Brady's room.

The door was closed. She tapped on it lightly. "Are you decent?"

"That depends on if you're making a moral judgment or a physical one."

He sounded somewhat exasperated. Now what? Erin rephrased her question, "Are your clothes on?" A breeze from the open window in the living room traveled up her back, making her shiver. She had to remember to close it before they left.

"That also depends."

This time, it sounded as if he was answering with his teeth clenched. Curious and more than a little anxious to get going, Erin gave up being polite. It took approximately half an hour to drive from here to Marlene's Newport Beach home, and they were swiftly running out of time.

"I'm coming in," she announced, turning the knob. "Now, can you—" Erin momentarily forgot about her dress as his reflection bounced back at her from the wardrobe mirror. God, he was handsome. He was also annoyed. "What are you doing?"

Brady's tie hung from his neck like two black, rumpled streamers that had outlived their usefulness.

He was about ready to toss the tie into the wastebasket. "Are you sure I've worn this before?"

"You always had trouble with your tie." "Always" comprised the one time she had managed to talk him into wearing a tuxedo for her friend's New Year's Eve party a year ago, but he didn't have to know that. With skilled fingers, Erin began to form a bow tie out of the mangled ends. "Don't worry about it. Men aren't very good at this sort of thing."

That sounded like a typical female thing to say, he thought. But the thought came fondly. He watched her fingers in the reflection. Damned if she didn't do it. "If they're not very good at it, why do they bother wearing one?"

"That's easy. To give the women in their lives a reason to feel superior." Patting the bow tie, Erin stepped back to survey her work. "There. You're gorgeous."

"No," he contradicted, his eyes sweeping over her. "You are." He saw her exposed back in the mirror. "But aren't you just a little drafty?"

Wise guy. "That's why I came in." Erin turned and presented her back to him, waiting. "I need you to zip me up."

It was a very nice back, he decided, the kind that tempted a man to run his fingers along it. Had he? Had he done it often? Or had he been too busy, the way she seemed to imply?

He realized that she was still waiting. Taking the two ends of the material, he maneuvered the zipper up to the top. "What would you do if I wasn't here?"

"Wear something else." Erin turned, adjusting her dress so that it fell more smoothly along the outline of her hips. "I can't exactly go knocking from door to door, hoping someone will zip me up."

"Why not?" He grinned, his eyes meeting hers. "It's a lovely back."

"Thank you," she murmured. "But it's not exactly meant for show-and-tell."

Her mouth quirked in a smile, but there was something he couldn't quite read in her eyes. Had he inadvertently said something wrong? "You're looking at me funny."

Erin shook her head. "Not funny, just appreciatively." Because he'd never been quick to give her compliments. She'd always read things into his words before. Now he was saying them and she enjoyed the transformation immensely.

She stepped back and looked him over one last time. There was no doubt about it, the man was a heart stopper. "You look good enough to stand on top of a cake."

He supposed that was meant as a compliment. He *felt* like something that would be found on top of a wedding cake. Brady looked himself over critically in the mirror. He looked all right, he supposed, but he would have been a lot happier in jeans and a T-shirt.

"I don't feel very comfortable." He moved his shoulders restlessly beneath the confining jacket.

Erin took his hand, leading him out of the bedroom. "You're not supposed to," she told him cheerfully. "It's a wedding. All men feel uncomfortable at a wedding." Her purse was on the hall table. She grabbed it as she passed. "I think it has to do with commiserating with the groom."

He took her word for it.

"They don't look very unhappy to me." Brady leaned forward and whispered the words to Erin just as they were shown to their seats by an usher. "They don't look unhappy at all."

He glanced toward the front of the large living room. Sullivan Travis and Dennis Lincoln stood side by side to the left of the minister, nervously waiting for the women they loved to walk down the aisle and permanently into their lives.

On the far right sat a small, thin gray-haired woman surrounded on three sides by bassinets, all gaily decorated with pink and blue streamers. It certainly was a family affair, Brady thought.

Erin took her seat, then waited until Brady was next to her. She inclined her head toward his. "What?"

He nodded toward the grooms. "You said I was supposed to commiserate with them. Looks to me as if they're pleased as all hell."

Erin looked at the two men. She recognized each from the glowing descriptions Marlene and Nicole had given her. A trace of envy wafted through her.

"Yes," she agreed softly. "They do."

Brady heard the wistfulness in her voice and looked at her thoughtfully.

The eternally familiar strains of "Here Comes the Bride" suddenly filled the air. From her place on the aisle, Erin had a good view of both Marlene and Nicole as they descended the stairs. It was hard to say which woman was more radiant.

At the foot of the stairs, they were joined by an attractive older woman dressed in Wedgwood blue chiffon. Her resemblance to Marlene was unmistakable. Even at this distance, Erin could see that she was blinking back tears. Beaming, the woman linked an arm with each bride and together they walked slowly down the long white satin runner to meet the minister.

"Who's that?" Brady asked, whispering the question into Erin's ear.

His breath tickled her skin. She shivered as the warm sensation wound all through her body. That hadn't changed any, either, she thought with satisfaction. Brady was still the only man who could set her on fire with just the slightest touch.

"That's their mother, Laura Bailey."

"Oh." On the way over Erin had explained all about the woman's recent reappearance after a twenty-year absence, knitting it into a story that was filled with misunderstandings, Justice Department investigations and a manipulative father who had made everyone's life a living hell while he'd been alive. It seemed to Brady that the Bailey women were way overdue for some happiness.

And by their expressions, he judged that they were well on their way to achieving that goal.

Erin looked over her shoulder at Brady. He was watching the ceremony thoughtfully, a hint of a smile on his lips. He looked, she thought, as if he was enjoying himself. The thought warmed her.

She couldn't tell which sister looked more beautiful. Marlene, tall, willowy and blond, was wearing a traditional floor-length bridal gown with a long veil that trailed after her. There was an incredible amount of appliqué on the bodice, and it ran the complete length of the veil. Erin wondered how Marlene had managed to get such an elaborate gown in such a short amount of time.

Nicole, shorter, with dark hair, wore a knee-length, long-sleeved white dress. The back was completely scooped out, showing off her bare skin.

Both women looked breathtaking.

The ceremony was relatively brief, but nonetheless moving. Both couples had written their own vows. The words were simple, the sentiment eternal.

Erin felt her eyes moistening. She couldn't help wishing that she was the one standing there, waiting for Brady to slip the ring onto her finger.

It'll happen, she promised herself. *Someday, it'll happen.*

As they rose to applaud the newly joined couples, Erin felt Brady's hands on her shoulders. He squeezed them lightly, mutely communicating his support. It was as if he knew what she was thinking.

But he couldn't possibly, she told herself. Brady had never been that intuitive. At least, she thought, turning to look at him, the old Brady hadn't been.

The reception was held at the house in a room that Erin could only speculate had been designed with huge celebrations in mind. No expense had been spared. Erin liked to think that her flowers, strategically positioned throughout the room, helped add to the mood.

There was a small orchestra playing on the side. People were dancing to the music, or sampling the various dishes from the long buffet table. Marlene confided to Erin that she'd been so impressed with the food at Dr. Pollack's uncle's restaurant where they'd attended a Christmas party that she had asked him to cater the wedding.

Erin looked around the room and saw several of the women she had become acquainted with in the doctor's waiting room. Dr. Pollack was there, standing off to one side, having a conversation with Marlene and Nicole's mother.

The doctor, Erin realized in surprise, was pregnant.

"I guess she got into the spirit of things," she murmured to Brady.

He handed her a glass of punch and took one for himself. "Who did?" He looked around to see who Erin was talking about.

"My doctor. She's standing over by the fireplace, talking to Marlene's mother. She's pregnant," Erin added incredulously.

Brady turned to look at the woman Erin had described. His eyes settled on a regal-looking blonde who most definitely had the rosy glow of upcoming motherhood about her.

"Must be something in the water," he quipped, taking a sip of the punch.

"Erin, Nicole just told me." Like a gust of warm summer wind, a bubbly auburn-haired woman swept over to them, squeezing Erin's arm.

Brady noted that like Erin and several of the other women at the wedding, she was pregnant. He began to wonder if it really *was* something in the water.

Mallory looked from Erin to Brady. "You look exactly the way she described you."

Brady laughed, amused. "Well, that's good. And you are?"

"Completely without any manners," she concluded. Inclining her head, she put out her hand. "I'm Mallory Flannigan." The handshake was firm and with feeling. She looked as if she was really glad to learn of his return. "Erin's had a really tough time without you," she confided to Brady.

It hadn't been anything Erin said so much as *how* she had said it. In her heart, Mallory empathized. Except that in her case, she knew there would be no happy resolution. But this was no time to dwell on that. A wedding was no place for dark, sad feelings, especially not in the face of a reunion.

Mallory turned to look at Erin standing at her side. "This is the first time I've seen her smiling since I met her."

Brady looked at Erin. He found it difficult to imagine her without a smile on her face. She was far too exuberant.

Someone called Mallory's name. She quickly swung around, homing in on the source. Delighted, she turned toward Erin and Brady again.

"Oops, I've got to go. I think I may have interested Nicole and Dennis in a cute little fixer-upper not too far from here." She winked at Erin. "Wish me luck."

The next moment, she was gone.

Like a streak of lightning, Erin thought fondly. "Mallory sells houses," she explained to Brady.

"I kind of figured that one out on my own." His mouth curved in an amused smile.

Behind them, the orchestra began to play a soft, dreamy tune. On impulse, Brady took the glass of punch from her hand and placed it beside his on the table.

He put his hand out to her. "Care to dance?"

Her fingers curled around his. The question surprised her. She was about to tell him that he didn't dance, but refrained. Instead, she asked, "Can you?"

"I don't know," he said honestly. He took her into his arms. "Let's find out."

It was as good an excuse as any to be in his arms, she thought. And right now, she wanted to be. Very much.

As the music surrounded them, Erin let herself drift with it. He danced very well, she observed. She wondered if he had always known how and had resisted, or if someone had taught him during his four-month absence. She thought of Demi.

Erin looked into his eyes, unable to remain silent any longer. "You don't like to dance, you know."

Brady shrugged. He had no recollection of what he might have told her. All he knew was that this felt right, swaying with her in his arms. And he seemed instinctively to know what to do.

"Maybe I just said that. This feels nice." He looked into her eyes. "Very nice."

"No argument here." He tucked her hand within his, holding it to his chest. Erin leaned her cheek against his chest. She could feel his heart beating.

It didn't get any better than this, she decided.

"Erin?"

His voice seemed to drift into her consciousness. "Hmm?"

He'd been thinking about them a great deal in the last week, trying his best to remember. He needed more information. "Were we happy?"

Erin raised her head, caught off guard by the question. "Yes, why do you ask?"

It was hard to put into words. He had a feeling that words weren't his medium. "I just wanted to know." He paused for a second, mentally stumbling. "It's just so hard, not remembering. Wanting to."

He was trying to reach out to her over a chasm, and as yet, their fingers hadn't managed to touch. She understood. "Don't force it. It'll come."

But what if it never did? he wondered. He had to make a life for himself now, not wait until he could remember. "If we were happy, why didn't we ever get married?"

That was a very good question. One that she had asked herself over and over again in the dead of night. She gave him the excuse she'd given herself. "You never got around to it. You were always so busy with work, you couldn't find the time."

He shook his head. Just how backward had he been? "That doesn't seem right."

"You had your reasons." It was a strange discussion to be having. She was defending his actions against his criticism. Normally, she would have found herself on the other side of the debate.

Whatever his reasons had been, they weren't good enough now. As he held her, he could feel the baby kick against him. His baby, he thought. It was time to stop searching for himself and live up to his responsibilities, even if he couldn't remember the way they had been arrived at.

"Let's do it."

He'd lost her. They were already dancing. What was he referring to? "Do what?"

"Let's get married."

7

Her throat was completely dry. For a moment, the entire roomful of people, food and music faded, leaving her alone in a darkened room with just Brady. Erin had dreamed about hearing those three words from him for so long. But the timing was all wrong now.

Gradually, the room returned, and with her voice. "You can't be serious."

It wasn't exactly the answer he had expected. "On the contrary, from everything I've been learning about myself, I am a very serious person." He frowned a little at the image he was forming of himself. He was a little too conservative, a little too predictable. "Maybe too serious," he added. "But whether that's true or not, I am serious now. Will you marry me?"

Erin didn't know whether to laugh or cry. She did neither. Instead, she stopped dancing with him and walked away.

Definitely not the reaction he would have expected, Brady thought.

Completely clueless, he hurried after her. He didn't have far to go. She'd stopped by the banquet table to get a cup of punch.

Brady touched her arm. "What's wrong? I thought you'd be happy." Was there something else he didn't know about? "Don't you want to marry me?"

Erin held the cup in both hands, staring into it as she gathered her thoughts, looking for the right words. Another woman might have played it coy, or close to the chest. Erin could only be herself.

"Yes, but not for the reason you're doing it. You don't love me. At least," she amended, "not right now."

At this point, he wasn't sure what love was, but he did know he was attracted to her. And maybe something more. Despite that, there was something more important at play here. There was a baby on the way. Soon.

He slipped his arm around her shoulders. "I'm working on it."

That was exactly her point. Erin shrugged off his arm. "Love isn't something you 'work on,' Brady, it just happens."

Brady looked at her with a patient smile. "I think we're going to have one of what you call our 'differences of opinion' on this. I happen to think that love takes a great deal of work."

"Once it's there," Erin agreed. Didn't he understand? She didn't want him marrying her out of a sense of obligation, and that was exactly why he was doing it. "Not before."

He approached this situation the way he had been dealing with problems at the lab. Methodically and with logic. "Erin, if this baby is mine—"

"If?" she repeated incredulously. Did he think that she would lie to him about something so important? Just what sort of a woman did he think she was? This was heading down the completely wrong path. "This baby *is* yours, Brady Lockwood," Erin said flatly. "There's no question of that." She hadn't even looked at anyone else since Brady had first come into her life.

Erin realized that her voice had gone up an octave. She sighed, lowering it. "But I guess you wouldn't know that."

In a way, he did. There was something about her that told him she wouldn't lie, wouldn't have betrayed him with another man. She had looked too overjoyed to see him that day in the restaurant. And there was love in her eyes, as well as pain.

"Sorry, wrong word. Just a transition to get me from one place in the sentence to the other," Brady assured her. "*Since* this baby is mine," he rephrased, "I want to take full responsibility for it."

He was making it so difficult to stick to her principles. "That doesn't include marriage to its mother."

His hand on her arm prevented her from walking away. "To me, it does." He said it with such conviction, she looked up at him in surprise. "That much I know about myself."

Erin pressed her lips together, wavering. No, it wouldn't be right. She couldn't do it, not this way. "Maybe I don't want to marry you," she countered.

He wasn't angry and he wasn't hurt, but he wasn't going to take no for an answer, either.

"Then you're being selfish and depriving the baby of its birthright," Brady told her quietly. "A baby deserves to have a mother and a father in-house. On call, twenty-four hours a day—"

He made it sound as if parents were synonymous with physicians. Or an all-night pizzeria. Erin held up her hand before he could continue spewing out analogies. "All right, all right. You've made your point."

"Then you'll marry me?" He searched her eyes for the answer.

This was all wrong, she thought. If she agreed, she would be taking advantage of her condition. What sort of way was that to build a marriage? She didn't want it to begin this way.

But you do want it, a voice whispered within her. *With all your heart.*

And maybe, bound to Brady before God and the state, she would find a way to really make him love her. After all, she had succeeded at it once, why not again?

A hesitant smile lifted the corners of her mouth as she nodded. "All right. Yes, I'll marry you."

Taking the cup out of her hands, he took both of them in his. "When?"

She almost laughed out loud. Tunnel vision. That sounded very much like Brady.

"Well, not now," she told him. Glancing in the minister's direction, Brady appeared unconvinced. Erin could almost read his thoughts and began to tick off the reasons why not. "We need blood tests, rings, a place to get married."

While she knew she couldn't very well have a traditional white wedding, she didn't want to exchange vows in front of a judge at city hall, either. Even the simplest of weddings required some planning. About the only thing she knew she didn't have to worry about was a bouquet.

"All right, a week then," he revised. It would be cutting it close, he thought, glancing at her abdomen. "That should give us enough time to make arrangements." When he raised his eyes to hers, Brady could see a glimmer of sadness in them. "What?"

"Nothing." Erin lifted a shoulder and then let it drop again carelessly. She didn't quite carry off the pose of nonchalance. Brady was obviously still waiting for an answer. "A woman who's been proposed to usually gets kissed within five minutes of the proposal." She was being silly, she thought. After all, this was Brady, whether he remembered or not. Brady didn't do things like kiss in public.

"Oh." Despite the people all around them, Brady took Erin into his arms. "All right."

His mouth curved in a smile as he touched his lips to hers. But one touch beckoned to another, until he had deepened it and completely disoriented both of them.

Erin's head swam. She struggled to maintain control. This was definitely *not* like Brady. He would have never kissed her with people around, much less with enough feeling to threaten to incinerate the clothing from her body.

When he released her, Erin could hear her blood rushing in her ears, drowning out everything else. She took a deep breath, trying to steady her erratic pulse. Her eyes were filled with surprise. And pleasure.

Feigning nonchalance, Brady glanced at his watch. "Made it. And with three and a half minutes to spare, too."

Erin could only laugh as she shook her head. Maybe this would work out all right, after all.

The telephone was ringing as she turned her key in the lock. Erin didn't have the faintest idea who could be calling her at this hour. Terry had closed the shop over an hour ago.

"I'll get it," Brady volunteered.

He hurried over to the telephone in the living room. When he lifted the receiver to his ear, he heard Erin's voice. Her answering machine had just clicked on.

"Hold on," he instructed whoever was on the other end of the line. "Don't hang up. Erin just has to get her spiel over with."

Spiel? Erin looked at Brady as she placed her purse on the coffee table. Since when did he talk like that?

Brady had always been so precise in his language. He'd always avoided slang of any kind, saying it wasn't dignified. *Spiel* was a word she used.

Yes, he was definitely different. She smiled to herself as she momentarily leaned against the arm of the sofa, waiting to see who was calling.

Brady waited until he heard the beep before he said anything else. "Hello? Are you still there?"

"Brady? Hi, it's Gus. I've got some good news for you." Hearing his friend's voice, Brady glanced at Erin. He had good news of his own to share with the other man, he thought. "We found your car."

Surprised, Brady covered the mouthpiece as he turned toward Erin. She was kicking off her shoes. Why did he find that so sensual? "It's Gus. He says they found my car."

She hurried over, her bare feet sinking into the carpet. That was a surprise. She'd been certain they would never see his automobile again. "What condition is it in?"

He shrugged in response. He hadn't thought to ask. It occurred to him that he didn't even know what his car looked like.

"What condition is it in?" Brady repeated into the receiver.

There was a pause as Gus considered the question. "Well, except for a dent on the passenger side, I'd say that it seems to be in pretty good shape."

Erin looked as if she was waiting for an answer, so Brady repeated what Gus had told him. "The only damage is a dent on the passenger side."

With relief, Erin waved away his words. "That was there before. You misjudged a parking space." Brady looked at her dubiously. She blew out a breath, recanting. "All right, *I* misjudged a parking space."

"That sounds more like it." By his own observation, he was too careful a driver. If a space appeared too small, he didn't test his abilities by angling into it. He just chose another one farther away.

How could he know her that well without knowing her? Erin wondered. It made her believe more than ever that it was only a matter of time before his memory returned. It was there, hiding in the recesses, just waiting to emerge.

The small, exasperated look that came into her eyes at being found out made Brady smile. "So, where do I go to pick it up?" he asked Gus.

"It's down at the police impound. Why don't I come by and get you?" Gus suggested. "That might be easier all around." He hadn't seen Brady since Brady had stopped working at Demi's restaurant. Gus was curious to find out how he was getting along. The ride over would give them a chance to catch up.

"Great." Erin raised an eyebrow in response to Brady's enthusiasm, but for the moment, he let her wait for an explanation. "When?"

"How does tomorrow sound?" Gus suggested. "Say, about three?"

That wouldn't work. "Can't, I'm working at the lab again." He was almost on a full schedule now. Things were coming back to him in dribbles. He had no memory of acquiring the information that rose whenever he needed it. It was just there. He supposed he should be happy with that, but there was still this restlessness within him to *know*. To know everything that had come before that day in the alley. "I get off at five-thirty."

"That's right. Demi and I have missed you at the restaurant, you know. How's the job going?"

Brady knew what Gus was asking. He wasn't making small talk about work. Brady sighed, but the level of frustration he had felt earlier just wasn't there anymore. "Still no revelations, but I seem to know what I'm doing at the lab."

It was rather uncanny, to have this huge deficit in his memory bank and yet still have his entire education at his fingertips. That, at least, seemed to be on automatic pilot.

"How's Erin?"

Brady smiled. "Fine." His eyes shifted to her. The smile broadened. "Say, Gus, would you like to be best man?"

"Best man at what?"

Brady crossed his arms before him, resting the receiver against his ear and shoulder. "My wedding." He waited for a flutter of nerves to hit him as he said it. It didn't come. Nothing seemed to be able to nudge away the contentment. He relaxed, pleased.

"You're kidding!" There was genuine surprise on the other end. "You're getting married?"

Gus couldn't have sounded more astounded than if he had told him that his memory had returned, Brady thought. "It seems like the right thing to do."

Erin slipped off the sofa and went to pick up her shoes. *The right thing to do.* Brady's words echoed in her head as she retreated into the family room. That was Brady, all right. She could always count on him to do the right thing.

Dropping her shoes in the coat closet, Erin sighed. The right thing. If that lacked the thrill and the romance she was hoping for, well, it wasn't as if it was a surprise. She knew Brady. He wasn't into romance and the trappings that went with it. She had been secretly hoping that he might be, somewhere down deep. She'd thought that it would surface now, without the hindrance of a set pattern of behavior. The kiss at the wedding had been misleading. He hadn't changed that much.

Romance often faded, she reminded herself. Her sister had been swept off her feet with long, romantic walks, candlelit dinners and idyllic weekends. The marriage had lasted barely eighteen months, falling apart after the proverbial first blush had faded from the rose.

That wouldn't happen with Brady. He was too clear-eyed, too dependable. If she didn't have romance, she did have a man who was pure gold.

She just wished it would shine a little more once in a while.

Brady stood beside Gus as Erin walked slowly around the Volvo. The car was dirt-encrusted, with mud all but blotting out the navy blue paint job. But she recognized the license plate as well as the make and model.

"It's your car," she assured Brady, turning around to face the two men. "Did you find anything in it?" she asked Gus.

"If you mean his wallet or his suitcase, no." Gus shook his head in further reply. "Just a few empty beer cans and a lot of cigarette butts. Whoever stole the car was a chain smoker."

Hey, buddy, got a light?

Brady felt Erin's hand on his arm. "Brady, what's the matter? You're pale."

He blinked, coming to. "Nothing. I thought I remembered something, but..." He shook his head. "Never mind."

She looked at him, uncertainly. All the color had momentarily drained from his face, but it was returning now by degrees. Her hand still on Brady's arm, she looked at Gus. "Where did you find it?"

"It was abandoned in one of the parking lots at LAX." Since its reconstruction several years ago, the airport had become so huge, it was difficult to hone in on one lone car that hadn't been picked up. "One of the guards finally noticed that it hadn't been moved for a while. He called his boss, who notified the LAPD. They ran it through the computer and came up with a match.''

That went along with her theory that whoever had mugged Brady had taken his plane ticket and used it. She tried to contain her frustration. The bastard had sent her on a futile search to St. Louis and cost her and Brady months of separation. If she had filed the missing person's report here, Gus would have seen it and brought her and Brady together sooner.

Brady inspected the car, rounding it slowly. He couldn't remember selecting it or driving it. He opened the driver's side and slid in behind the steering wheel.

Nothing.

He glanced toward Erin. She was watching him, hopeful. He felt worse for her than for himself these days.

''Now you won't have to drive me to and from the lab.''

I don't mind doing that, Brady, she thought. She liked seeing him off to work, liked picking him up from there. Liked having him back in her life.

Brady got out again, still looking at the vehicle. It was a sturdy neat-looking little car, the kind that he would have guessed he would purchase. Nothing fancy, just reliable.

Gus gave him a clipboard to sign. ''Just a formality,'' he explained, indicating the signature line. ''So what's this about a wedding?'' He handed the clipboard to another policeman.

Brady and Erin had made a few arrangements since coming to the decision yesterday. Erin had told Brady on the way home this afternoon that it had taken her all morning to convince her minister that she knew what she was doing. With reluctance, the man had agreed to officiate. Erin considered it a coup. At least she wouldn't have to face city hall and its impersonal atmosphere.

"It's this Sunday. The minister is marrying us in his vestibule. So how about it? Do you want to stand up for me? I can't think of anyone I'd rather ask. Besides—" Brady's mouth quirked as he looked at Gus "—you're the oldest friend I have."

They *had* become friends, Gus thought. There had been a bond forged between them since that day he had found Brady wandering in the alley.

Visibly touched, Gus offered Brady his hand, sealing the bargain. "Hey, the pleasure's all mine. Just make sure the maid of honor is pretty."

Maid of honor, oh wow. Erin's mind scrambled madly. She hadn't thought of that. Terry, she would pick Terry. She was as close to Terry as she was to anyone.

"I'll see what I can do," she promised Gus. They had to be going. If she had a wedding to arrange, she was going to need every scrap of time she could muster. Erin looked at the car. "Is there gas in it?"

"Enough to get you to the gas station on the corner," Gus answered.

"Then that'll have to be my first destination."
Brady got in behind the wheel again.

"We didn't find the keys in the car," Gus informed
him.

"No problem." Brady dug into his pocket and pro-
duced a set. "Erin had spares."

Gus looked at Erin with appreciation. "Someday,"
he said to her, "I'd like to find a woman just like
you."

"It might be cheaper just to carry a spare set of
keys." Erin grinned at him. She had no idea how a
man as good-looking as Gus had managed to remain
free all this time. Strictly by choice, she imagined.

Erin looked at Brady, unable to still the nervous
flutter she felt. She laid her hand on the steering wheel
before he could turn on the ignition.

"Why don't you wait until I pull my car around?"
she suggested. "So you can follow me home."

He read the look in her eyes. "Afraid I'll get lost?"

There was no point in lying. "Yes." She said it so
seriously, she surprised both of them.

"Okay," Brady agreed easily. "I'll wait."

This wasn't the way she'd envisioned it, Erin
thought as Brady brought the car to a stop in the
church's parking lot. This wasn't the way she'd envisioned her wedding day. She looked at him. But he was
definitely the person she had envisioned marrying.

Brady pulled up the hand brake and then sat for a
moment without getting out. She wondered if he was

having second thoughts. Since his disappearance, there was a part of her that was braced for the worst. "Nervous?"

"No."

Oddly enough, he wasn't. He reflected on what she had said at the double wedding last week. If men were supposed to be naturally leery of this sort of commitment, maybe it was better that he had lost his memory. He felt as if pieces of his life were falling into place.

"Thanks for not making me wear a tuxedo." He got out of the car and rounded to the passenger side. He opened the door for her.

Erin took the hand he offered and got out. "Didn't seem right making you go traditional when I can't." She smoothed out the skirt of her dress.

He looked at the cream-colored lace dress she had selected the day before. She hadn't said anything, but he knew she'd had her heart set on a long, white gown. Maybe they could still do that eventually. He'd heard that people renewed their vows on anniversaries.

"You look very pretty."

She didn't feel very pretty. She felt dowdy, but she appreciated the compliment.

"Thanks." As he began to walk toward the church, Erin tugged him back. "Are you sure you want to go through with this? There's still time to back out."

She was protesting a little too much. Maybe there was more to it than he realized. Maybe she really didn't want to marry him and couldn't bring herself to say it. He searched her eyes for an answer.

"Do you want me to?"

"No," she said seriously. "But I don't want you to regret it, either."

He looked into her eyes and knew she was telling him the truth. Still holding her hand, he smiled as he rubbed his thumb over her knuckles. "I won't."

For his sake, she vacillated a moment longer. But she had loved Brady from the moment she'd set eyes on him. She couldn't force herself to refuse, even if it would have been noble of her.

Noble only went so far.

Taking a deep breath, she flashed him a smile. "Okay then, let's do it."

As they walked from the rear of the lot, Erin saw a beige sedan pulling in on the far side. She could make out two people in the front seat. The car drew closer until the driver parked right next to their car.

Gus got out of the driver's side, as Demi emerged from the passenger's side.

"Hi," Demi called out, waving. She hurried to join them, leaving Gus behind to catch up. "I hope you don't mind, but I made him bring me. I just love weddings," she explained.

Counting Demi and the minister, there would be six of them if the minister didn't bring his wife. "Even tiny ones?" Erin quipped.

"Especially tiny ones." She smiled warmly at Erin. "It makes it exclusive. And afterward, I'm hosting your reception in the banquet room at Aphrodite's. No argument," she added when Brady opened his mouth.

Demi talked almost as fast as Erin, Brady thought. And jumped to conclusions just as quickly. "I was about to say thank you."

"Oh." She grinned. "That you can do." She looked around. "Where's the maid of honor? Gus said she was cute."

"I said I *hoped* she was cute," Gus corrected as he joined the group. He shook his head, looking at Brady. "She never listens." Demi poked him in the ribs.

Erin looked at the main road leading to the church, searching for Terry's car.

"Terry usually cuts it kind of close," Erin said. Although for once, she mused, it would have been nice if she was early.

The next moment, a compact red car came barreling into the lot, screeching to a halt beside them. Terry popped up like blond toast out of the driver's seat. The car had barely come to a stop.

"Hi, sorry I'm late," she apologized breathlessly. "I had to speed all the way—" She took a look at Gus, suddenly recognizing him. "No, I didn't," she corrected herself.

Gus grinned. "I'm here unofficially," he assured her. "I heard nothing. Especially not the squeal of tires."

Terry flushed and laughed, then looked at Erin. "Gosh, Erin, you look great."

Erin looked down at her hugely expanded waistline. "I feel great."

"Not that kind of great," Terry admonished. "Terrific great." Helpless, she looked at Brady for support. "Tell her."

Brady lifted his shoulders and let them fall again. "I already did."

"Then tell her again," Demi prompted.

Brady exchanged looks with Gus, amused. "We're outnumbered."

"Tell me about it. I have been outnumbered all my life. C'mon," he urged. "Let's get you two married."

"Oh, wait, I almost forgot." Terry hurried back to her car and pulled out a beautiful bouquet she had arranged. "For the bride."

Erin took the bouquet and looked at it lovingly. "It's beautiful."

"And so are you," Brady assured her. "Let's go make a wedding."

Erin nodded. That sounded wonderful to her.

8

Erin stood in the doorway of her bedroom, watching as Brady walked down the short hallway to the room he had been occupying for the past two weeks. It didn't seem right for him to remain there, since they'd been married today.

She bit her lip, debating whether to say something. She didn't want to do anything to jeopardize the mood that surrounded them.

The reception at Aphrodite's had been wonderful. Demi had outdone herself decorating it, even though there were only five of them. She'd even had the chef bake a small, three-tier wedding cake. One of the waiters had used Erin's camera and taken photographs to commemorate the occasion. Erin had secretly been upset that her parents and sisters weren't able to attend her wedding on such short notice. But all the wonderful treatment from people she hardly knew helped negate the underlying sadness that pervaded her.

The five of them had remained in the restaurant's banquet room and talked for hours. Terry spent a good deal of that time flirting with Gus, who flirted right back. Erin discovered that she really liked Demi, and Gus had turned out to be very entertaining. Time had passed very quickly.

When it was over, husband and wife had returned home to her condo. Erin was in a state as close to euphoria as she thought was legally allowed.

And now it was time to begin living the rest of her life. She didn't want to be the first to make the suggestion, but in light of the fact that they were now husband and wife, she thought they should be sharing the same bed.

Erin cleared her throat. "I think," she began, choosing her words carefully, "seeing as how we're married now, that maybe we should sleep in the same room."

Brady turned around without skipping a beat. Those were his sentiments exactly, but he hadn't wanted to seem insensitive to her condition. He assumed that perhaps she preferred sleeping alone at a time like this. Obviously, he'd been wrong.

He brushed a kiss over Erin's lips as he passed her on the way into the room. "I think you're absolutely right."

Entering, Brady looked around. This was the first time he'd been in her room. The first time he *remembered* being in her room, he amended silently. Given her personality, he'd half expected to see kickknacks and clutter on every surface. But the room was amazingly neat and spacious. Even the window seat had only pillows strategically arranged on it.

She seemed to favor white, he noticed. The bedspread was white eyelet, and there were white curtains at the windows. He felt an aura of peacefulness as he looked around. What he didn't feel, to his disappointment, was a sense of familiarity. Not on any level.

This wasn't the time to dwell on that, he told himself. It would come. Eventually, it would come. Brady drew back the covers and got into bed. He tucked the covers around his waist and, smiling invitingly, waited for her to join him.

Erin's eyes traveled over the length of his bare chest. He had always hated pajama tops. How many times had she seen him just like this? And yet, it seemed like the first time. Erin couldn't help feeling just a little nervous.

Like a bride, she mused.

She slid into bed hesitantly, then propped herself up on her elbow. *Poor Brady.* "Not exactly what you had in mind for a wedding night, is it?"

It wasn't something he had given much thought. There had been too much else to concentrate on. Had they ever discussed what married life would be like for them? he wondered.

Following her cue, he propped himself up on his elbow and faced her. "Actually, I don't know what I had in mind for a wedding night."

He was just being kind, she decided. Another plus in his favor. She thought of the night ahead and frowned. There was absolutely no way for her to lie down beside Brady without looking like a human version of Mount McKinley.

"Most men don't envision their wedding night lying beside a woman who's about to give birth."

Brady laughed at her serious expression. "Now there you have me."

Erin searched his eyes, trying to find the answer in them. "Do I, Brady? Do I have you?"

Why did she sound so unsure? He had married her, hadn't he? Maybe it was a pregnant thing. Brady smiled at her reassuringly. "That's what it says on the license."

He didn't understand. "I'm not interested in a license, Brady. I'm interested in what goes on in here." She tapped his chest.

To answer, he took her hand and spread it across his chest, then covered it with his own. His heart was just beneath her palm. "You tell me."

"I don't know." And then she grinned at him mischievously. "It's beating."

She was in it, he thought. He just couldn't find the words to tell her. Or maybe he just wasn't ready to say them aloud.

"Yes, it is." He looked at her seriously. "For now, I think that's the best I can expect. I can't say how I feel until I know the rest of it. I do know that I'm looking forward to this baby."

Erin's eyes widened as she stared at him. Now *that* was a surprise. "Are you?"

She looked almost startled. Why? "Sure, who wouldn't be?"

Given his previous feelings, she wasn't convinced he meant what he was saying now. Maybe he only thought he did, or was saying what he thought she wanted to hear. Or, like their wedding night, maybe he hadn't really given it much thought at all.

She looked for an analogy he could relate to. "You know, babies aren't like physics books. You can't just shove them on a shelf when you're busy or don't feel like bothering with them."

He smiled at the comparison. Maybe, unknowingly, she had picked the right example, after all.

"I never shove my books anywhere, and I'm rarely too busy for them. I like having them around." He touched her cheek lightly and felt a desire building that he couldn't do anything about for some time to come. But he could assuage her fears. "It'll work out, Erin. I'm not too sure how just yet, but it'll work out."

Now there was a first, him comforting her. It was a day of wonders, Erin mused. "I thought you weren't an optimist."

"I'm not." A smile played on his lips. "But I've been keeping company with one." He kissed her forehead. "They say the best traits usually rub off."

Almost nine months pregnant and she felt desire curl in her veins like scented smoke. "Is that my best trait?"

"That..." He grinned. "And you're a hell of a kisser." Brady glanced at the clock on the nightstand next to Erin's side of the bed. "I've got an early day tomorrow." He needed to be in at seven. He looked at her ruefully. "I guess I should have taken some time off." This was a hell of a time to think about that, he upbraided himself. He really was behaving like an absentminded professor.

Erin shook her head. "That's all right. You were gone for five months. You can't exactly take a week off now."

She never ceased to amaze him. "And you're all right with that?"

He looked relieved, she thought. The old Brady had expected her to make concessions. This one was surprised by them. She slid her hand over his. "You're beside me, Brady. I'm all right with everything."

"You're one special lady, Erin Lockwood." He liked the sound of his name following hers. "Did I ever tell you that?"

For some, Erin thought, that would have been a rhetorical question. For Brady, it was one he wanted an answer to.

She shook her head, savoring his remark. "Not until now."

He looked down at her ring. She had opted for a plain, simple band, but there was nothing simple about her. He touched it lightly with his fingertip. "I was pretty slow."

"Oh, I don't know." She thought of the things that had drawn her to him. "You were kind of endearing in your own way."

Given the evidence, he hadn't arrived at the same conclusion. "I worked long hours, didn't take you dancing even though you wanted to go." He had seen that much in her eyes at the wedding reception last week. "Didn't tell you what you needed to hear—" He looked at her, mystified. How did a man get to be so lucky? "Why did you stay with me?"

She had already told him. "Because I loved you."

That didn't answer his question. He had to know. If he knew why she had remained, maybe that would be the key to understanding himself. "Why?"

Not everything had an answer. "Because I just did," she said softly. Amusement shone in her eyes. "You can hypothesize and explore a thing to death, but in the end there's that tiny X factor." She couldn't explain it any better than that. "It's either there, or it's not. If it's there, you love someone." She ran her fingers lightly along his face. And she did. She loved him very, very much. "If it's not, nothing you can do will make it be there."

He still didn't understand. But then, he was beginning to think that approaching this logically wasn't the way to go. He smiled at her fondly. "Sounds like a lot of illogical double-talk to me."

She laughed, kissing him. "It would. To you. But it works for me."

He pulled her into his arms. "Maybe it works for me, too." Nestling her against him, Brady lowered his mouth to hers.

Instant fireworks. Instant desire. The kiss flowed through her like overheated lava and made her wish she wasn't so pregnant. She ached to make love with Brady the way they used to. The way they hadn't nearly frequently enough.

She wound her arms around his neck, bringing him closer, losing herself in the pleasure his mouth could create for her. Erin sighed with frustrated contentment as he kissed first one lid and then the other, working his way along her jaw and pressing a kiss to her throat.

The magic was very much there.

"I am *really* looking forward to this baby," Brady murmured against her lips.

He wouldn't be, she thought. If he remembered who and what he had been, he wouldn't be. Her heart raced, accelerated by the wonders his lips were generating. "Why?"

"So we can really get this marriage under way." Pregnant or not, the sexual pull he felt toward her was enormous. It was one he had no intentions of fighting once the baby was born. But it went beyond that. Maybe it wasn't logical, but he did feel as if she was his soul mate. As if they were meant to always be together.

Banking down the demands desire had created within him, Brady settled back on the bed. He curved his arm around her, resting his head against hers. "I might not be able to make love with you tonight, but at least I can hold you until we both fall asleep."

To her everlasting pleasure, he did.

Erin stood shifting from foot to foot at the front door. She frowned self-consciously as she looked at Brady. He had curtailed her quick getaway. "You don't have to do this, you know."

He had come home from work to find Erin on her way out, a pillow tucked under her arm. She was going to her Lamaze class. Brady relieved her of her pillow, asking for five minutes, just long enough to grab an apple and get ready.

"Don't have to what?" He checked for his car keys. He wondered if he had been this absentminded before the mugging. "Come to the class?"

She shrugged carelessly. She didn't want him feeling obligated to accompany her. She didn't want him feeling obligated about anything at all. That wasn't the cornerstone upon which she wanted to build her marriage. "The class . . . and the delivery room."

He found his keys right where he'd put them, on the coffee table. Brady turned around to look at her. "Why, don't you want me there?"

She let out a frustrated sigh. Lately, as her due date approached, she was getting edgier and edgier. "No, it's not that. I just don't want you to feel that you have to do any of this."

Brady had always been a stickler for obligations and responsibilities. To her, that sounded too much like being shackled. The last thing she wanted was for Brady to feel imprisoned by her or anything connected to her. She wanted him to do exactly what he was doing, but because he wanted to, not because he had to.

Can't have your cake and eat it, too, she thought ruefully. Just having him along should have been enough to make her happy.

Brady tucked her pillow more securely under his arm. "Well, if I'm going to be in the delivery room, I should know what's going on." He looked at her, waiting for her to challenge him. "That's only logical, right?"

She bit her lip. The other classes had all taken place during her lunch hour, but the instructor had had a conflict and rescheduled this last one in the evening. She'd come this far on her own. And it had been damn lonely.

"Yes, but—"

He opened the front door and held it for her. "Don't argue with me, Erin. Just get in the car." Brady led the way to the Volvo, but she hesitated at the door. "Now what?"

She toyed with the handle. "Are you doing this because you feel you have to?"

"Yes." He paused after throwing the pillow into the back seat. "I can think of sights I'd rather witness than you screaming and wracked with pain," he told her honestly.

She'd asked for it. "Then why do it? One of us going through this is enough." She looked down at her stomach. "Since I seem to be rather committed to this, you get the option of not having to be there."

He didn't want an option. He wanted to be there for her. "I was there with you in the beginning—even though I can't remember—and I'll be there with you at the end. It's only fair."

Since she still wasn't getting in, he walked around the hood and came to her side. He opened the door for her.

She didn't care about fair, she only cared about feelings. And his were just as important to her as her own. Maybe more so.

"But—"

Very gently, he opened the door and ushered her into the seat. "And I figure you need me," he continued as if she hadn't protested. "That's reason enough for me." He pulled the seat belt out as far as it could go, then offered it to her. "Now, are you going to buckle up, or are we going to be late?"

She took the belt from him and slipped the metal tab into the slot. "I'm buckling up."

"How about that," he murmured as he got in on the driver's side. "An argument I finally won. Is this a first for me?"

Erin looked at him. "No. You convinced me to marry you," she reminded him.

Brady started the car. "I don't think I had to push that hard." He glanced at her as he pulled out of the driveway. "Did I?"

"No," she admitted after a beat. "Not very hard at all."

"Okay." He took a left turn down the block and headed toward the street that led out of the development. "Now that that's settled, directions?"

Erin settled back in her seat. "The class is being held at Harris Memorial Hospital. Make a left at the light." She pointed to it needlessly. Erin, he had already learned, liked to talk with her hands. And he liked to watch.

The stars were out in full regalia when they walked out of the hospital two hours later. Class had run over. Since it was the last session, the instructor had wanted to review a few things with them. Even so, Erin felt far from prepared.

Brady lingered by the car, studying the sky. It was a beautiful night. He didn't want to go home yet.

"Are you up for a stop?" he asked.

Erin looked at him, puzzled. He had never liked staying out late during the week. It interfered with work. "Isn't it getting late?"

"Yes, but I noticed this little outdoor café on my way home tonight. It's new." Or maybe he'd never noticed it before. "The sign in the window says they're open until nine. It seems like a perfect night to sit out and watch the stars." He looked at her. "Are you game?"

It took her a moment to assimilate his words. This *really* was out of character for him.

"Brady, it's forty-five degrees out." Or thereabouts, according to the weather report they'd heard on the radio while driving to the hospital.

Forty-five degrees didn't feel that chilly, he thought. It felt bracing.

"You've got on a coat," he said. He closed the top button for her, then lifted the collar. "It just seems like too pretty a night to end, that's all."

The look in his eyes warmed her. His attitude warmed her. Romantic. The word whispered across her mind. Brady was being romantic. "Even after the video the instructor showed?"

Several men, as well as a few of the first-time mothers, had turned a very vivid shade of green during the video. Erin had expected Brady to get up and take a walk down the corridor until the video was over. Instead, he'd sat beside her on the folding chairs that had been set up for the screening, holding her hand throughout the fifteen minutes they viewed the tape. It was incredible how safe she felt with him there.

"Maybe I'm trying to put the video behind me," he confided. His expression became serious as he looked at her. He certainly didn't envy Erin the ordeal that lay ahead of her. "Seems like an awful lot of pain to endure."

"Thanks." She laughed shortly, though a smile was harder to muster. "I needed that."

He hadn't meant the words to come out that way. "Sorry, pretty tactless, huh?"

The fact that Brady recognized how his words must have sounded to her and apologized really stunned her. He just wasn't the same man who had disappeared from her life all those months ago. The last few weeks had been like living in a dream. Living *with* a dream.

If she were to describe him to anyone, she would have said he was the new, improved Brady. Like detergent that had been tinkered with. Except he was a human being. A fantastic human being. She prayed that things wouldn't change again any time soon. She liked him just the way he was.

Erin inclined her head. "Apology accepted. As well as the invitation. I'd love to try out the new place." Her eyes lit up. "Maybe get some hot chocolate if they serve it."

"Hot chocolate it is," he promised.

"With whipped cream?" Erin added, sliding into her seat.

He got in. "So much, you won't be able to lift the cup."

Erin grinned. "Oh, I think I'll manage."

The stars seemed to circle around them as they sat, nursing their drinks of choice. It was a cool, crisp evening that braced cheeks and made a man feel glad he was alive. Alive, he thought, as he looked at Erin, with the right woman.

They were the only patrons sitting outdoors, though there were several nestled around small, circular tables within the coffee shop. Erin surrounded the mug of hot chocolate with her hands, drawing on the warmth. If she wasn't already in love with him, she mused, she would have fallen in love with him tonight.

Maybe she was right, Brady thought. It was getting chilly. He didn't want her getting sick so close to her due date. "Too cold for you?"

When she looked up from her mug, she smiled contentedly. "No, I've got my hot chocolate and you, not necessarily in that order. I'm just fine." Erin raised her eyes to the sky. "You're right, it really is a pretty night."

He could watch her all night, Brady thought, this woman he knew so little about. He set down his cup and reached for her hand.

"Tell me about yourself, Erin. Tell me things I don't know." That, he realized, covered a lot of territory. "What were you like as a child? Did you like spinach when you were growing up? Did you have crushes? Did you hang up posters over your bed and write fan letters to rock stars who never answered?"

She held up her hand, stopping the onslaught of questions. They had been together a little over two years when he had disappeared. He'd never wanted to know any of this. She had told Brady about herself before, but it had been on a volunteer basis. It had amounted to spoon-feeding him the information. He'd never asked for it and never looked particularly interested in knowing. He'd been content to let her talk when she wanted to and not question anything.

The fact that Brady wanted to know these things now warmed her far more than the hot chocolate.

Erin sat back in her seat. "I have two sisters, both older. My parents live in Washington—the state, not the capital. I hated spinach, still do, but we can't let the baby know that," she interjected. "And I never put up any posters or wrote any fan letters. I was never particularly struck by anyone." She leaned over the table, her eyes holding his. "Until there was you."

That was what made it all hard to believe. She was vibrant, alive, bubbly. He was the exact opposite. "Me? I'm the dry, scientist type."

The one thing that hadn't changed an iota was his modesty. He was the same unaffected man she'd always known. He had absolutely no idea of the effect he had on her, or other women when they looked at him.

Erin nestled her chin on her upturned hand, still looking into his eyes. "Still waters ran deep, and I wanted to go wading in them."

And he wanted to have her wade. As soon as possible. But right now, he had more questions that needed answers. "How did we meet?"

"How did we meet," she repeated as the memory rose in her mind. "It was raining. My umbrella had just turned inside out. You offered to walk me to my car." She'd been struck by his chivalry. And his terrific profile.

Brady looked at her incredulously. "You trusted a perfect stranger?" Of course she did. Erin seemed to trust everyone to be just like her.

"You had nice eyes." Mischief lit hers. "And you weren't all that perfect."

He shook his head. Though he found it endearing, being too trusting was one of her flaws. "Ted Bundy had nice eyes, too."

"Really?" She pretended to be fascinated. "I never met him. But I did want to meet you." From the moment she first laid eyes on him.

"Why?" he prodded.

"Because I had a feeling you were the right one, the one I had been waiting for." She saw the question coming. "Women know these things."

He laughed, getting into the spirit of the story. "More illogical logic?"

"Exactly." She took another sip before the chocolate grew cold. "Anyway, you walked me to my car, but it wouldn't start. I'd left my lights on and the battery was dead," she explained. The knowing look in his eyes was a familiar one. "You walked me back to the mall so I could call a towing service," she continued. "While I waited, we had sandwiches at one of those little restaurants around the perimeter." She looked around. "Kind of like this one, except it was a lot noisier." She looked at him. "I paid for the meal to thank you for being so nice."

Erin drained her mug, then placed it on the table, fitting it over the ring it had formed. "Then we went out to wait for the driver to arrive. By the time he did, you had asked me out." She saw the thoughtful look on his face. He might as well have the truth. "Actually, I asked you out because you were too slow."

That sounded just like her, he thought.

"I told you I had two tickets to the revival of *Cats* and no one to go with. At the time, it was playing at the Performing Arts Center."

Brady finished his coffee. "And did you?" he asked. "Have tickets?"

She grinned. "You catch on fast. No," she admitted. "But I did after I finished talking to you. I called the box office and ordered tickets that afternoon as soon as I got home." With a languid sigh, she pushed away the mug. It felt wonderful just to be alive. "Anyway, that's the story of how we met." She peered at his face. "Any of this coming back to you?"

He shook his head. "No." It was still as if there were a brick wall between him and his memory. Nothing more had returned to him since he had begun working at Edmond Labs. But he had ceased feeling so restless, so frustrated by the situation.

Instead, he was satisfied just to enjoy what he had. And Erin.

Brady pushed his chair back. "Ready to go home, Erin?"

Erin nodded as she moved the chair away from the table. Home, she mused, rising. It had a good sound to it.

9

Two more customers walked out of the shop, one after another. Erin sighed as the door closed. Behind her, Anthony was taking three more arrangements to load onto the delivery van. Her head was throbbing, and her body felt as out of sync as was humanly possible. It felt like the longest day of her life.

Erin rubbed a hand over her forehead and turned just as Terry hung up the telephone. "Boy, I can't *wait* for this day to be over."

Terry picked up the two order sheets Erin had just written out and added the one she'd taken over the telephone. She leaned into the back room and handed all three to Juanita, her eyes on Erin.

"What a strange thing for a sentimental woman to say on Valentine's Day." She took a sip from the can of soda she kept beside the register. "Especially a sentimental woman who owns a flower shop." Her expression softened to one of sympathetic concern. She looked at Erin's stomach. "Baby acting up?"

Acting up was putting it mildly. For the past two days it felt as if the baby was practicing to stage its own revolution, automatic weapons and all.

She laughed softly, taking Terry's soda can from her. Erin took a long sip before answering.

"I wish he or she would hurry up and get here to lend a hand." She returned the can to Terry. The soda didn't help. Nothing was going to help until the baby was finally here. "I can't remember a more hectic day." There hadn't been time for either of them to break for lunch, so Erin had sent out for pizza instead. The last slice was sitting very heavily in her stomach. "This is even worse than all those orders last Mother's Day."

"Worse?" Terry echoed.

Erin waved a hand in suppressed exasperation. "You know what I mean. Crazy. Hectic."

Erin turned, looking at the glass where they kept their flowers on display. They were going to have to start using those pretty soon. Anticipating a rush— everyone always waited until the last minute—Erin had doubled her usual order from the nursery. It was just about depleted now.

Everyone, it seemed, was in love this year. Not that she blamed them. Erin smiled to herself. Being in love was wonderful. If anything, it was entirely under-rated.

Terry studied her best friend thoughtfully. "You know, you didn't have to come in today. After all, it is your due date." She nodded toward the back room.

"I could have had Juanita call her cousins. We would have handled the orders."

Erin knew that, but it was beside the point. She needed to be here, to keep busy, so that she didn't dwell on how miserable her body felt today.

"I couldn't just sit home and listen to my skin stretch. Besides, I thought that this might induce labor." Something had to. She would just die if she was overdue. Waiting nine months had been bad enough. Waiting a minute longer came under the heading of inhumane.

Terry looked at Erin anxiously. "Oh, thanks, thanks a lot. You know I faint at the sight of blood."

Erin laughed, shaking her head. She took another vase from the display. Juanita had used the flowers in it to fill the last order she'd taken. "Just what I need. Support."

She heard the door opening again and looked quickly around the showroom. She hoped whoever it was wasn't going to ask for red carnations. They were completely out of them. Erin heard the delivery truck leaving. It had gone out a record number of times. Anthony was chafing to get home to his own girl, but they still had a couple of hours left before they closed up.

Provided they didn't completely run out of everything. Erin placed a bouquet of daisies into the vase and turned around to place them on the counter.

"Hi."

The vase almost slipped from her fingers when she saw Brady. She looked at him with apprehension as he greeted Terry.

"Anything wrong?"

Her eyes searched his face. Had his memory returned? she wondered suddenly. What else would have brought him here at this hour? He was supposed to be at work. Brady *never* left work early.

She looked flushed, he thought. The pink blush to her cheeks was enticing. "Absolutely nothing."

"But you're here, and it's—" she glanced at the clock on the wall directly above the glass display "—five o'clock."

He grinned as he looked at the clock. "Guess you won't have to be going in for an eye test any time soon." He looked at Terry before continuing. The woman nodded imperceptibly. Good. "Seeing as how you refuse to give birth today, I came by to take you out to dinner."

"Dinner?" Erin repeated dumbly. Brady didn't care for going out to eat. He claimed the food never tasted right to him. She had to keep reminding herself that this was a different Brady.

Brady took her hand, coaxing her out from behind the counter. "You know, where they use knives, forks, talk a little. I hear that it's really catching on in some regions."

"I know what dinner is." Behind her, Terry made no attempt to stifle a giggle. Erin looked over her shoulder reprovingly. "But why are you taking me out?"

He got a kick out of the way she treated everything with awe and wonder. Obviously he hadn't been a very attentive lover, he mused. But that had been a mistake he was about to change.

"Haven't you heard?" He tapped a drawing of Cupid hanging over the display. "It's Valentine's Day. You're supposed to do something special for your valentine today." Brady extended his hand toward Terry in what Erin realized was a rehearsed gesture. "Terry, flowers."

From beneath the counter, Terry pulled out a small arrangement of violets and baby's breath. Erin's favorites.

"Flowers," Terry announced.

"Flowers," Brady repeated, handing the bouquet to Erin. He watched her take them, her hand closing around them as if she had never seen flowers before. "I know this is like a busman's holiday for you, but—" He stopped and lifted her chin with the crook of his finger. "Erin, are you crying?"

She didn't answer him. She couldn't. All she could do was nod as she stared down at the bouquet, which blurred before her eyes.

He slipped his arm around her shoulders. "Is it the baby, Erin? Are you having contractions?"

Pressing her lips together to seal in the sob, she shook her head.

If it wasn't the baby, it had to be him. He didn't understand. What had he done wrong? "Then what? Tell me," he coaxed.

Erin blew out a breath, struggling to steady her voice. She hoped it wouldn't crack when she answered. "You've never given me flowers before."

Brady wouldn't know about that. He could only guess that perhaps he had thought it was a little redundant, bringing flowers to a florist. Obviously, whatever his reasons, they had been wrong. Dead wrong.

"Then I should have," he said softly. He took her hand in his, drawing her toward the door. "Are you ready to go?"

Guilt pricked her, warring with a desire to be with him. She really wanted to go, but she had obligations, just as he did. Erin looked back at Terry. She couldn't just leave her manning the shop on a whim.

"But I haven't closed the shop yet," Erin protested.

Terry waved Erin toward the door.

"Don't worry about a thing. If you'd acted normally in the first place and given birth today, I'd be running the show, anyway. There are only a couple of hours left. Juanita and I can handle everything." Terry inclined her head so that her voice carried to the back room. "Can't we, Juanita?"

A small, dark-haired woman of about forty stuck out her head from the rear of the store. She was holding the last of the pink roses, which she was fashioning into an arrangement that was destined for the glass vase on the worktable.

"Is she still here?" Juanita looked at Terry incredulously. "I thought she was supposed to have gone by now." She shook her head in disapproval as she looked accusingly at Erin.

Erin exhaled loudly, but there was no missing the pleasure in her eyes. "That's what I love, support from the people around me," she murmured to Brady.

In reply, Terry handed Erin's shoulder bag to Brady and gestured toward the door.

Brady threaded the strap onto Erin's shoulder, ushering her along. "C'mon, I've got reservations for us for five-thirty."

He *was* serious. "Where are we going?" As if she didn't know.

"Aphrodite's." It seemed appropriate, seeing as how this was also their one-week anniversary. "Gus said he might drop by later," he added.

She laughed, twirling her bouquet in her fingers. "How romantic."

Romance. Of course, she wanted a romantic dinner. How romantic would it be for her if there were other people present, he thought ruefully. "If you don't want him to—"

Erin laid a finger to his lips, freezing the apology. The man was almost too perfect, she thought. "No, it was a joke. I like Gus. Demi, too." She knew it was important to him that she like his friends, and she was glad that she could be honest about it.

"You can always send him here," Terry called after them as they walked out the door. "I could use a curly-headed Greek with eyes like midnight in my life."

The door closed behind them. "She likes him," Erin told Brady.

His car was parked at the curb. He ushered her over to it, then opened the door. His eyes glinted. "How can you tell?"

Humor, she thought. He had a really nice sense of humor. That hadn't been in plentiful supply the first time around.

The first time around. The phrase echoed in her head. It sounded as if she had had him recycled. In a way, she supposed he had been. The best parts had remained, augmented by a whole new side of him that had never been there before.

Erin couldn't help wondering just how much would remain once Brady remembered everything.

For the first time since Brady had returned, she wasn't all that certain she wanted him to remember. Perhaps it was selfish of her—perhaps?—but she had to admit, at least to herself, that she really did like him better this way.

"You're awfully quiet," Brady remarked as he drove down MacArthur Boulevard. At this hour, the traffic was heavy. It had absorbed his attention for a while. He glanced at Erin now. Was she feeling ill? "That isn't like you."

No, she supposed it wasn't. "I'm counting my blessings."

"Now that *is* like you." It hadn't taken him long at all to realize that she was optimism personified. "What's the total?"

Lightly, Erin placed her hand on his arm. He glanced at her as he made a left turn. "Oh, I'd say it's way past infinity."

Infinity. He looked at her face and knew she actually meant that. "Do I fit in there anywhere?"

Was he serious? Erin stared at his profile. Yes, he probably was. "You're right at the top of the list. You're what makes it infinity."

Erin sucked in her breath as another strange twinge hit her unexpectedly. Wow, this baby had a kick like a mule with steel-tipped boots.

Maybe this wasn't such a good idea, Brady reconsidered, looking at Erin's expression. Maybe he should just take her straight home and order in. "What's wrong?"

It was all right now. Erin blew out a breath, steadying herself. He looked really worried, which she found endearing. It also made her feel guilty. Erin shook her head. "Just a twinge."

Normal people had twinges. Pregnant women did not have twinges on their due date. They had warning signs. He debated turning around and going home. "What kind of twinge?"

She could tell by his tone what he was thinking. "Relax, this has been going on for two days now. It's nothing, just another pain to add to the ever-growing list.'' Erin ran her fingers along the swell of her stomach. Right about now, her abdomen felt as if the skin was stretched to its limit. "Having a baby might be natural, but it's certainly not fun."

No, he didn't suppose that carrying one around for these last few months had been easy. Still, he liked the idea of her having a baby. Their baby. "Do you want to have any more children?''

More children. More swollen ankles. More morning sickness. More pain. Yes, probably. She grinned. "Let me have this one, okay, and I'll get back to you on it." The meaning behind his question suddenly hit her. She stared at him. "Why, do you?"

He turned into the parking lot behind Aphrodite's, examining the idea. "I think so." Brady parked between two sports cars, pulling up the hand brake. He sat for a moment, thinking. Imagining. "One thing I know for sure." He smiled at her. "I definitely want to remember getting to that state the next time around."

The words all but seduced her. She had a feeling in her heart that this Brady was a better lover than he had ever been. It certainly was something she was more than willing to find out.

She couldn't believe the change that had come over him. Erin grinned to herself as Brady opened the door for her.

"Want to let me in on the joke?" He extended his hand to her. Erin wrapped her fingers around it and drew herself up slowly to her feet.

She supposed it was time to tell him everything. It was only fair. "You know that argument we had the last day?"

Her phrasing amused him. "You mean the one you said was about nothing?"

She supposed she had that one coming. "Yes, that's the one. Well, it wasn't about nothing." She took a breath to fortify herself, for once hoping that what she said wouldn't trigger anything in his mind. "It was about having children."

There was something in her voice that alerted him. "What about having children?"

Erin looked up at the sky. There were no stars tonight. She would have thought there would be on Valentine's Day, so that lovers could stop and make a wish. She licked her lips. There was no way to work up to this.

"You didn't want any. You told me that you thought the world wasn't a place that you wanted to bring children into."

That sounded awfully callous to him. He tried to imagine himself saying something like that to her and couldn't. "But you were pregnant then."

"Yes, but you didn't know that," she reminded him.

He felt awful for her. Brady took her arm as they walked toward the restaurant. He could imagine just how she must have felt, hearing him say something like that.

"It must have been terrible for you." She nodded. "How did you put up with me?"

She had no difficulty answering that, especially not now. Stopping on the steps before the restaurant, she touched his cheek. She hadn't thought that she could ever love anyone as much as she did then, but she loved him even more now.

"Because I loved you, remember?"

Brady remembered because she had told him. He just didn't understand why, despite her little explanation about the "X factor." From the pieces he had put together, he sounded pretty damn stuffy.

Her words played themselves in his head like a delayed message. "Loved?"

Erin twirled the bouquet he had given her in her fingers. Terry, bless her, had placed the stems into a tiny plastic receptacle filled with water, and then subtly camouflaged it so that she could keep the flowers with her tonight. Terry knew how Erin's mind worked.

Erin raised her eyes to his. "Love," she amended. Maybe she should have waited until he told her first, but she had never been one to hold back. She didn't now. "I love you."

Incredibly moved, Brady threaded his hands through her hair. "And I—"

"Hey," a loud voice boomed, shattering the moment. "Sorry to break up this little conversation, but are you going in there, or what? We'd like to get some dinner before we grow old."

Brady and Erin turned to see a heavyset man standing behind them. An embarrassed-looking woman was on his arm. She shrugged a mute apology.

"We're going in," Brady told him, taking Erin's hand. He pulled open the heavy wooden door.

She wished that the man had made his appearance just a minute later. A minute would have been long enough for Brady to tell her what she wanted to hear.

So much for hearing the words, Erin thought, resigned. Maybe later.

Please, later.

As she stepped inside the restaurant, the warm air immediately caressed her like an old friend. It was heavy with the scent of aromatic food mingling with the smell of candles and the presence of bodies.

Erin opened her coat, feeling a little too warm. Brady was leading her toward the back. It seemed very crowded tonight, she thought, looking around.

"We have the best table in the house," he assured her, bringing her to a booth. He laid the "reserved" sign facedown on the edge of the table. "Away from the kitchen and the meandering traffic." He waited until she had taken her seat before sliding in opposite her. "Tonight, I want you to myself."

"I think Gus might have other ideas." Erin nodded behind him. Brady turned around to see that Gus was on his way over.

"Oh." He had completely forgotten about Gus. Brady wanted a few minutes alone with her to finish what he had started saying at the door. "I can send him off."

She was touched that he offered. "In his own sister's restaurant? I don't think so."

Besides, there would be time to be alone later. Right now, she just wanted to savor this completely new side of him. Brady hadn't particularly enjoyed socializing before, and she enjoyed watching him with Gus, enjoyed the lighter side the other man brought out in him.

Gus joined them, surprising Erin with a small box of chocolates. "Oh, boy, more calories," she teased. "Thank you, Gus, but shouldn't you be saving this for your own girl?"

"By the time I find one, the candy will be stale," he assured her. "You keep them." He looked from Brady to Erin. "So, still no baby, eh?"

Erin shook her head as she looked down at her stomach. Another twinge passed through her like a swift-footed animal. She was pretty confident that she hadn't winced.

"I think he or she's decided that it's safer in here." Erin sighed. It was getting so that she couldn't remember not being pregnant. She turned the conversation toward more interesting things. "So, why doesn't a good-looking man like you have a date on Valentine's Day?"

"Too many to choose from," Gus quipped.

And none of them serious, he thought. Being the carefree bachelor was fun for a while, but now it had grown old. A lot of his friends were either getting married or already married and starting families of their own. Like Brady, he thought, looking at the man beside him. Oh, well, maybe his day would come soon.

"Poor baby," Erin teased. He could be settled in an instant if he really wanted to be, she thought. He was that type. Right now, she figured, he just really didn't want to. When he did, the right woman would be there, probably directly beneath his nose.

She shifted in her seat, wishing that there was a comfortable niche for her. But that continued to elude her these days.

"So, how's my favorite valentine couple?" There was affection in Demi's voice as she joined them. She nodded at her brother, her expression purposely solemn. "Gus."

It drew out a satisfied grin from him. "She always gets grumpy when she has to serve me," he confided to Erin.

Demi fisted her hand at her waist as she stepped back to look at her brother. "So, what's changed since we were kids?" She looked at Erin. "Gus always liked bossing me around."

Brady opened the menu out of habit, then closed it. He already knew what he wanted. The same thing he always had. He was a creature of habit. When he found something that he liked, he thought, looking at Erin, he stuck with it.

"It's good for you," Gus was saying. "Builds character."

Demi rubbed Gus's head. "Better to build it than to be it." She looked at the others. Brady had his menu closed and Erin hadn't opened hers. "So, what'll you have?"

Erin opened her mouth to protest that for once in her pregnancy, she didn't feel very hungry. But the words she was about to utter turned into a very audible moan as the twinge blossomed into something far more lethal, far more hot, twisting her into a knot.

Demi glanced around, hoping no one else heard. "Hey, the special of the house isn't that bad," she protested with a smile. Then her eyes narrowed. Even by candlelight, Erin's complexion had grown very pale. She took her hand. "Erin? Are you all right?"

She couldn't really answer that. "I'm not too sure," Erin heard herself saying quietly. Everything felt a little out of focus. "I—oh!"

Her skin felt clammy, then burning hot. For just a moment, the room became blurry. All she saw was the yellow flame flickering above the candle. The room was shrinking down to a pinpoint. She struggled to keep the darkness from engulfing her.

Erin.

Her name.

Someone was calling for her. No, to her.

The darkness retreated, and Erin realized that Brady was repeating her name over and over again. Concern. She heard concern in his voice.

She mustered strength from somewhere, attempting to smile at him. "It's okay. It's nothing."

"The hell it's nothing." Gus was sliding out of the booth, with Brady directly behind him.

"Cancel dinner, Demi," Brady told her. "It's time to take Erin to the hospital."

They were forgetting the most important player, Erin thought, struggling to focus on them. "Hey." Both men looked at her. "I'm the one who says it's time," she informed them.

Another very strange twinge began in her loins and ran a course down her legs, bearing down hard.

"Time," she breathed.

Gus nodded as Brady gently brought Erin to her feet. "I thought so." He buffered her other side. "Do you think you can walk?"

Without waiting for an answer, Brady picked Erin up in his arms. "She's not walking."

"I'm too heavy," she protested with far less feeling than she'd intended.

He wouldn't have expected her to show vanity at a time like this. He decided he still had a lot to learn about her. And he intended to, slowly, carefully. He figured it would easily take one lifetime.

"You haven't had dinner yet, so it's okay." Brady shifted her in his arms. He waited for Gus to lead the way out. "Demi, alert the hospital that she's on her way. Harris Memorial in Newport. And call her doctor," Brady added as an afterthought. "Dr. Sheila Pollack."

Even though she was in pain, Erin couldn't help being impressed. Brady actually remembered her doctor's name. "Very good."

He smiled at her. "I paid attention."

She winced again before she could answer.

"C'mon, Erin. I'll even let you run the siren," Gus said over his shoulder as he led the way.

10

Gus broke the connection with the dispatcher, then glanced into his rearview mirror. Brady had one arm around Erin. He was holding her hand with the other. From where Gus sat, it looked as if she'd cut off all circulation to Brady's fingers.

"Are you all right back there?" Gus asked.

Erin let out a breath as another contraction faded. If she bit down any more on her lower lip, it was going to resemble Swiss cheese.

"I've been better," she gasped. A lot better, she thought.

Brady tightened his hand on hers. Damn, he felt so helpless. It wasn't a feeling he was happy about. "Is there anything I can do for you?"

"You can get someone else to have this baby." She shifted, moving from side to side, trying to find someplace where the pain wouldn't find her. There was no such place. "I don't think I'm going to like this experience." Another contraction was beginning. Oh, God. "As a matter of fact, I'm sure of it."

After enduring two days of strange, fluctuating sensations zipping through her like stunted electricity, this was happening much too fast for her. And yet, not nearly fast enough. She wanted it to be over with.

"Demi called the doctor," Gus assured her for what was probably the third time. "I'm sure she'll be at the hospital by the time we get there."

Brady looked out the window. He had his doubts about that. Gus was flying. The hospital was only minutes away. "Only if she lives close by."

Erin tried to concentrate on what was being said around her, and not on what was happening to her. A fragment of what the doctor had once mentioned in passing returned to her.

"She does. In the condominiums located just beyond the hospital." Erin gasped as another pain seized her. She pressed her lips together. "Boy, I really hope she's home tonight."

Gus brought the car to a screeching halt by the emergency-room entrance.

"We're about to find out," Gus announced as he got out quickly. He stopped long enough to issue an order. "Stay here." The next moment, he ran through the electronic doors.

Within two minutes, Gus returned with a nurse and an orderly following in his wake. The latter was pushing a wheelchair.

Brady squeezed Erin's hand just as Gus opened the door for her. "I guess this is it."

She felt damp all over. Her water had broken. Erin couldn't remember ever being this uncomfortable. "If it's not, I would hate to be here for the real thing."

Brady and the orderly helped her out of the car and into the wheelchair. Erin nodded her thanks. She didn't think she could have gotten out on her own power, much less walked.

"Mrs. Lockwood?" the nurse asked.

"Yes," Brady and Gus chimed together.

The nurse looked at them curiously. "Dr. Pollack's already here." They'd received a call from the doctor's service fifteen minutes ago telling them to be prepared for Erin's arrival. Exuding efficiency, the nurse edged in between Gus and the orderly with the wheelchair. "We'll take it from here, Officer, thank you."

Gus was reluctant to leave. "If it's all the same to you," he said to Brady, "I'll stick around."

"There's a waiting room on the fifth floor," the nurse told him. "It's meant for expectant fathers who don't want to be in the delivery room—"

Gus nodded. "Close enough."

"Thanks for getting us here, Gus. I'll keep you posted," Brady promised. He noticed that, despite the pain she was in, Erin was smiling. They were having a baby, he thought. They were really having a baby. Even with all the physical evidence, it still hadn't completely sunk in.

With an air of regained authority, the nurse turned to look at Erin sitting in the wheelchair. She took a clipboard from the desk.

"We'll just get you registered and then be on our way."

"Already done," Erin breathed, clenching her teeth. It was beginning to hurt really bad. "Last week." The last thing she wanted was to have to wait in a hallway while someone keyed in her health-insurance information.

The nurse let the clipboard drop back on the desk. She nodded at the orderly. "Then I guess we're on our way."

Yes, Erin thought as she watched the corridor walls pass by as they hurried to the elevator in the rear of the hospital, *they certainly were. But only one of them was in pain.*

She looked so drenched and exhausted, and he couldn't do a damn thing about it. The frustration that Brady felt rivaled what he'd experienced when he'd tried to remember a shred of his life.

The latter frustration had mellowed. He knew everything he needed to know, he decided. He knew he loved her, and that she was part of his life. She *was* his life. He had his whole world right in this room, in this hospital bed.

Anticipating her, Brady took a spoonful of ice chips and pressed it to her lips. But Erin shook her head, moving it away.

"No, that's all right. It won't help, anyway."

God, she'd never felt so drained in her whole life. Not even that time she'd gone hiking with her sister. They'd gone on a family camping trip, and she and Alice had accidentally misplaced the camp. They'd hiked for hours, trying to find their way back.

That had been a picnic compared to this. She had been in labor for over five hours. When she had arrived at the hospital, she'd been certain that the baby was going to come in a matter of minutes. The minutes had ticked by, feeding into hours and still no baby.

Erin exhaled a breath she had no energy to expel. When was it going to end? "No wonder they call it labor," she muttered to him. "I can't remember ever working so hard in my life."

"I'm sorry, Erin."

It was a moment before she realized he was holding her hand. The edges were getting very blurred in the last few minutes. No, the last forty-five, she amended, looking at the clock on the opposite wall. The clock whose minute hand constantly seemed to be getting stuck. It froze every time a contraction hit her.

"For what?" she asked after a beat. What could he possibly be sorry about? He'd been wonderful throughout this.

Brady drew the chair in closer to the bed and sat down. He took her hand in his again, covering it with his own. "For everything. For the pain you're feeling. For not remembering.'' He knew that had to hurt her, that he still couldn't remember their life together.

She wanted to reach up and smooth away the furrow in his forehead, but that would have taken energy she didn't have. ''You can't help, either.''

That wasn't quite the truth. He brushed the hair out of her eyes. It was plastered to her forehead with perspiration. ''I got you pregnant.''

She smiled weakly. He was blaming himself. How like him. She wondered if he knew that.

''Yes, but it's not exactly anything you planned.'' She looked at him, trying to remember. Had she told him this already? Things were getting muddled in her mind. ''As a matter of fact, you were very much against it.''

He wasn't now. Brady wanted this child. More than anything in the world, he wanted to hold his son or daughter in his arms. *Their* son or daughter, he amended silently. But if what she said was true, it raised another question. He knew she wasn't the type to be underhanded or go behind his back to get what she wanted.

''Then how—?'

That was exactly what she had asked herself when the home pregnancy test had turned out positive. She'd taken the birth control pills faithfully.

''Nothing's foolproof.''

He swept away one last strand from her forehead. ''I'm glad.''

Had she heard him right? There was this rushing sound in her ears. Her eyes searched his for verification. "Are you?"

He nodded, tightening his hand around hers. He could see the monitor from where he sat, the one that showed a contraction coming even before it hit her. Empathizing, he braced himself.

"I wish there was another way for us to have this baby," he told her, "but I'm not sorry that we're having it."

She was going to comment on the "we" part when she suddenly arched, squeezing his hand as another contraction caught hold of her. She hurried the words out, wanting to say them before she was in too much pain to form them.

"You don't know how happy that makes me. How much I've wanted you to want this baby."

Anything more had to wait. She couldn't think, couldn't speak. All she could do was pray.

And then, as before, the horrible pain receded. It was over. Temporarily.

But just as suddenly, another contraction, more fierce than the last one, materialized. She cried out in surprise before she could stop herself. Erin was determined not to scream. Other women might scream and curse, but she wasn't going to. Her baby wasn't going to be ushered into the world on a shriek. She bit down hard on her lip.

Concerned, Brady rose from the chair. Disengaging himself from her took a little more effort. "Erin, I'm going to call the doctor."

Erin shook her head frantically from side to side on the damp pillow. She didn't want Brady leaving her, even for a moment. She could get through this, as long as he was with her.

"It's too soon," she protested with as much strength as she could gather. The doctor had just been in to see her. "It's supposed to take longer." Although, if it took much longer, she was sure she was going to die.

Brady was unconvinced. Didn't one contraction on top of another mean she was ready to deliver? Damn, if this was an experiment in the lab, he would know what he was doing. But here, he was completely at a loss. "Maybe the baby didn't read the manual."

He left the room before Erin could call him back. Brady looked up and down the long, dimmed corridor. In deference to the holiday, there were hearts and red-and-pink streamers decorating the walls and doors. He hardly noticed any of it.

Dr. Pollack was at the nurses' station. She was on the telephone. As he drew closer, it was obvious that she was talking to a new mother, assuaging the woman's fears about the color of her son's umbilical cord attachment.

"It dries up before it falls off, Mrs. Nelson. No, really, it's all right. You don't have to bring him to the emergency room. It's supposed to look like that. Yes, yes, it is strange, but nothing to worry about." Noting the look in the nurse's eyes, Sheila turned to see Brady behind her. "Just a minute, Mrs. Nelson. I'm going to let you speak to one of our pediatric nurses. Please hold." She quickly surrendered the receiver to the woman beside her.

"Yes, Mr. Lockwood?" Sheila smiled reassuringly at him. "Any progress?" She thought it prudent not to point out that she had been in to see Erin only five minutes earlier. Expectant fathers didn't want logic. They wanted it to be over with.

"I think she's ready."

Sheila plunged her hands into the pockets of her white coat. She'd begun wearing it in the last month. It effectively covered her expanding silhouette. "All right, let's see."

Entering the room, Sheila took out yet another pair of sterile rubber gloves from the dispenser on the wall and slipped them on. She had to remember to ask the nurse to get her some hand lotion.

Sheila smiled warmly at Erin as she positioned herself at the foot of the bed. "So, Erin, ready to have a baby?"

At this point, Erin was beginning to doubt it was ever going to really happen. "I've been ready for the last month."

Sheila laughed. "Atta girl." She examined Erin quickly, then double-checked by feeling around the opening. Brady was right. It was time. "One hundred percent dilated," she declared, slipping the sheet back into place. "We have ourselves another opening and another show."

Pleased that Erin's ordeal was almost at an end, Sheila stripped off her gloves and discarded them in the wastebasket. She began to hum a tune as she crossed to the door. The locker room was only a few feet away from the delivery room.

Sheila glanced at Brady. "Oh, you need to get ready, too, Mr. Lockwood. Follow me."

Brady began to leave, then hesitated in the doorway, looking at Erin.

His thoughts were practically written across his forehead. Sheila took his arm, coaxing him out.

"She'll be fine," she assured him. "The nurse will take her to the delivery room." He followed her down the hall. "We have to get you sterile. Of course," she looked at him over her shoulder, "if we did that before, you might not be here."

Sheila stopped before the delivery room and smiled encouragingly at him. "Smile, Mr. Lockwood, it's going to be just fine. The baby's heartbeat is strong, and Erin's a healthy young woman. There's absolutely nothing to worry about." She opened a door to the narrow locker room reserved for fathers-to-be. "You'll find everything you need in there."

Brady nodded his thanks and went in, closing the door behind him. He changed quickly, the doctor's assurances echoing in his mind. She seemed so confident, but he knew that there was always a chance that something could go wrong. He couldn't help worrying. After finding his way back to her, he didn't want to take a chance on anything happening to Erin.

He supposed the matter was completely out of his hands and in a far bigger pair at this point.

Dressed in off-green livery, Brady pushed open the swinging door and looked around. He wondered if this was the way interns felt the first time they entered a delivery room. His stomach was queasy, and he was really looking forward to having this over with. For both their sakes.

Apparently, he'd beaten the doctor in, he thought. The nurse attending Erin looked up as he walked in and smiled at him. At least he assumed she was smiling. Her eyes crinkled above the blue mask she was wearing.

Brady crossed to the delivery table, taking Erin's hand. "Hi, stranger."

"Don't say that," she breathed. "Not strangers, not ever again."

He held her hand tightly. "Don't worry, we won't be."

Sheila entered through another door, leading in from the doctor's locker area. Her manner was bright and breezy, as if they were gathered for a friendly luncheon rather than the birth of a baby.

"Well, I see all the principal players are here." The nurse slipped a pair of gloves on Sheila's raised hands, then tied the ends of her mask on securely. Ready,

Sheila seated herself at the foot of the table. Something was missing.

She frowned, looking up. "Rachel, someone forgot to switch the light on today. I won't be able to see what I'm doing," she quipped.

The delivery room was bathed in lights, but the one directly behind her was off.

Apologizing for the oversight, Rachel turned on the switch. The incandescent bulb flashed as the filament, in a weakened state, burst from the sudden surge of electricity. Looking straight at it, Brady was nearly blinded by the flash.

A flash of lights. Bright lights. Headlights, coming directly at him.

The air in Brady's throat caught.

Tires squealed as they came thundering down a street freshly slicked by an unexpected afternoon rainfall.

In an instant, Brady saw himself, *felt* himself running, then tripping and falling. He was rolling on the pavement, desperately trying to get out of the way of the oncoming wheels.

His wheels. His car.

He was rolling, rolling, crashing into metal garbage cans, his head hitting a brick wall.

Then nothing.

Everything.

Brady's head snapped up as he heard someone calling his name. He wasn't in an alleyway. He was here, in the hospital delivery room.

Here with Erin.

"Oh, my God," he mouthed.

"Mr. Lockwood?"

Sheila had seen husbands and lovers grow pale, and some of them had even fainted in the delivery room during the birth process. This one looked as if he was about to go before the ordeal actually began.

"Mr. Lockwood," she repeated, raising her voice this time. "If you'd prefer waiting outside, I'm sure Erin will forgive you." She looked at Erin and smiled knowingly. "In time."

He was having trouble gathering his thoughts together. There was suddenly so much to sort out. "What?"

"The waiting room," Sheila repeated again. She looked expectantly at the nurse.

Rachel moved to his side, ready to escort him out of the room.

"No," Brady said heatedly. Still a little dazed, he looked from one woman to another, and then at Erin. "Wait. I remember."

Sheila exchanged looks with Rachel. She felt Erin stiffening and knew another contraction was coming. This was no time to begin a prolonged debate with the man. She could only guess at his meaning.

"The class. Yes, I'm sure you do remember, but right now I think you'd be better off if you—"

The doctor didn't understand. How could she? She didn't know. "No, I remember." He looked at Erin, urgency and elation rushing through him on twin chariots. "Erin, I remember. Everything." Every part of their relationship. The day he met her. Their last argument. It was all there for him to wade through and relive.

She would be a great deal happier right now if her body wasn't being ripped apart.

"Oh, Brady, that's wonderful, but right now, I think…we're…going…to…have a *baby!*" Oh, Lord, it hurt.

Sheila had no idea what was going on, but at least Brady didn't look as if he was going to faint anymore. "All right, Mr. Lockwood, if you're determined to remain, pick up her shoulders," Sheila instructed.

Brady immediately complied, propping Erin up gently. She felt so thin beneath his hands, he thought. When this was over, he was going to make it up to her, he swore. All of it.

"All right, Erin," Sheila said cheerfully, "you know the drill. When I say the word, I want you to push. Ready?"

"Now?" Erin pleaded. Every part of her body was begging her to push.

"No, not now," Sheila cautioned. "Breathe, Erin. Pant until I give the word."

Brady panted along with Erin, giving her a rhythm to adhere to. The doctor nodded her approval, then signaled. "All right. Now. Push!"

Brady counted down for Erin. As she bore down, he could have sworn he was pushing right along with her. Every muscle in his body tensed and tightened.

To Sheila's surprise and Erin's everlasting relief, the baby arrived almost immediately. Overjoyed, Erin collapsed onto the table.

"You have a girl," Sheila told them. Holding the baby by her ankles, Sheila examined the brand-new life that had fallen into her waiting hands. Perfect, she verified. "A beautiful, healthy baby girl."

"A girl," Erin whispered. Just as she had hoped. She blinked twice to focus as she watched the doctor hand her daughter over to the nurse. Her daughter. Jamie.

With her last shred of effort, Erin shifted her eyes toward Brady. "You remember?"

Or had that been part of the hallucination that had overtaken her?

"I remember." He looked at his daughter. "And always will."

"Oh, Brady," Erin whispered, tears forming. "I love you."

He felt as exhausted as if he had pushed the baby out himself. But not too exhausted to smile at the woman who held his heart in her hand.

"I remember that most of all. And that I love you." His eyes caressed her. "I just didn't remember to tell you."

Rachel placed his brand-new daughter in his arms. "But I will," he promised both of them. "From now on.'' Because you never knew just how much time you had, he thought. Or how lucky you were.

''She's seven pounds and two ounces,'' the nurse informed them.

''A 7lb., 2oz. Valentine,'' Brady marveled.

''Jamie,'' Erin said. ''We'll call her Jamie.''

''I can't think of a nicer gift to get for Valentine's Day.'' He looked at Erin. ''Thank you.''

She answered him with her eyes. Emotion had temporarily robbed her of the ability to speak. But he understood and would from here on in.

* * * * *

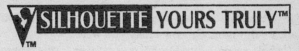

*Sneak Previews of March titles,
from Yours Truly*

It Happened One Week by JoAnn Ross
Amanda Stockenberg was in the middle of the worst
week of her life, looking like something the cat dragged
in and acting rather unladylike, when she saw *him*. Her
first love. And now she has only seven days for a second
chance at forever....

What Engagement Ring?! by Martha Schroeder
April Kennan had refused to even *date* attorney
Jake Singleton's brother, let alone marry him, but he
insists she broke their engagement and kept a four-carat
diamond ring! Now Jake's demanding she return a ring
she'd never been given—or else!

Don't miss...

MACKENZIE'S PLEASURE

by *New York Times* bestselling author
LINDA HOWARD

Mackenzie's Mountain. Mackenzie's Mission. In February 1996, bestselling author Linda Howard continues the Mackenzie family saga with *Mackenzie's Pleasure,* IM #691.

Zane Mackenzie was a soldier through and through. He was the best—the only man for the worst of jobs. Then he rescued sweet Barrie Lovejoy from her hellish captivity, and in the desperate hours of the night sealed both their fates. Because danger hadn't ended with Barrie's release. The enemy was still only a heartbeat away—even as Barrie felt the first stirrings of life within her....

Mackenzie's Pleasure—
the book you've been waiting for...
from one of the genre's finest, only in—

As seen on TV!
Free Gift Offer

With a Free Gift proof-of-purchase from any Silhouette® book, you can receive a beautiful cubic zirconia pendant.

This gorgeous marquise-shaped stone is a genuine cubic zirconia—accented by an 18" gold tone necklace.

(Approximate retail value $19.95)

Send for yours today...
compliments of ▼ *Silhouette*®

To receive your free gift, a cubic zirconia pendant, send us one original proof-of-purchase, photocopies not accepted, from the back of any Silhouette Romance™, Silhouette Desire®, Silhouette Special Edition®, Silhouette Intimate Moments® or Silhouette Shadows™ title available in February, March or April at your favorite retail outlet, together with the Free Gift Certificate, plus a check or money order for $1.75 U.S./$2.25 CAN. (do not send cash) to cover postage and handling, payable to Silhouette Free Gift Offer. We will send you the specified gift. Allow 6 to 8 weeks for delivery. Offer good until April 30, 1996 or while quantities last. Offer valid in the U.S. and Canada only.

Free Gift Certificate

Name: _____

Address: _____

City: _____ State/Province: _____ Zip/Postal Code: _____

Mail this certificate, one proof-of-purchase and a check or money order for postage and handling to: SILHOUETTE FREE GIFT OFFER 1996. In the U.S.: 3010 Walden Avenue, P.O. Box 9057, Buffalo NY 14269-9057. In Canada: P.O. Box 622, Fort Erie,

---

FREE GIFT OFFER
079-KBZ-R

ONE PROOF-OF-PURCHASE

To collect your fabulous FREE GIFT, a cubic zirconia pendant, you must include this original proof-of-purchase for each gift with the properly completed Free Gift Certificate.

079-KBZ-R

HOW MUCH IS THAT COUPLE IN THE WINDOW?
by Lori Herter

Book 1 of Lori's Million-Dollar Marriages miniseries
Yours Truly™—February

Salesclerk Jennifer Westgate's new job is to live in a department store display window for a week as the bride of a gorgeous groom. Here's what sidewalk shoppers have to say about them:

"Why is the window so steamy tonight? I can't see what they're doing!"
—Henrietta, age 82

"That mousey bride is hardly Charles Derring's type. It's me who should be living in the window with him!"
—Delphine, Charles's soon-to-be ex-girlfriend

"Jennifer never modeled pink silk teddies for me! This is an outrage!"
—Peter, Jennifer's soon-to-be ex-boyfriend

"How much is that couple in the window?"
—Timmy, age 9

HOW MUCH IS THAT COUPLE IN THE WINDOW?
by Lori Herter—Book 1 of her Million-Dollar Marriages
miniseries—available in February from

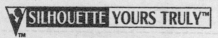

Love—when you least expect it!

LHMILLION

You're About to Become a *Privileged Woman*

Reap the rewards of fabulous free gifts and benefits with proofs-of-purchase from Silhouette and Harlequin books

Pages & Privileges™

It's our way of thanking you for buying our books at your favorite retail stores.

Harlequin and Silhouette— the most privileged readers in the world!

For more information about Harlequin and Silhouette's PAGES & PRIVILEGES program call the Pages & Privileges Benefits Desk: 1-503-794-2499